the TOR TRILOGY

TOR
ASSASSIN HUNTER

by

Billy Bob Buttons

With pen and ink drawings by Teri Smyth

the WISHING SHELF press

ISBN 978 - 1530114757

Edited by Alison Emery, Therese Råsbäck and Svante Jurnell.
Pen and ink drawings by Teri Smyth, www.terismyth.com.
'Tor' and 'sword with flower' on dustjacket by Laura Tolton,
www.laurajanetolton.wordpress.com

For my sister, Vic, who I lost,
and for my son, Albert, who I never will.

'If you kill a man, they will call you 'Assassin', if you kill a hundred men, they will call you 'Conqueror', but if you kill everybody, they will call you 'God'.'

Beilby Porteus (clergyman) 1731-1809

'Swedish history is the history of her kings.'

Erik Gustaf Geijer (poet) 1783-1847

'It is a man's own mind, not his enemy's, who tempts him to evil ways.'

Buddha 624 BC

'Evil needs only a timid victim.'

Ayn Rand (writer) 1905-1982

Tuesday, 1st September, 1870

18 Days to Assassination Day

0533 hours, Northern France

A bullet ricochets off a 16th century French cabinet, splintering the shiny walnut top. I duck and muster a lopsided grin. I know, any moment now, hundreds of howling German troops will storm our flimsy barricade of stools and rusty iron bathtubs, but I still think the cabinet would look wonderful in a scholar's study or in a quaint villa in southern Italy…

'SIR!' The shout jolts me back to the horrors of war. 'The scout the French sent out just reported in. He spotted the enemy holed up in the Hôtel Le Château Fort just up the Rue

de l'Eglise.'

This from my second-in-command, Jasper: crew cut, three gold teeth, tattoos of bottoms and boobs from his wrists to his elbows; he's a Goliath of a man from Ullapool, which, according to him is a 'dump of a town' in the very north of Scotland.

'He spotted a full regiment of the rats, Major; mostly cavalry.' He thumps the metal foot of a chipped bathtub. 'When they hit this wall of yours it will topple like a domino.'

I remember the hotel well: pretty archways, silk sheets on the four-poster beds and a rose-entwined balcony overlooking a sunny courtyard, now just a jumbled hill of bricks and charred wood like the rest of La Moncelle. The town had been so sweet, the home of soft cheese and the fruity Neuf-de-Pape wine, now the home of black crows enjoying a banquet of French trooper eyeballs.

'Jasper, lad,' I punch his iron-cast bicep, bashing my knuckle; he has the tree trunk-sized limbs of a century old chestnut, 'if…'

My second-in-command grunts. He's no fool.

I relent. 'Ok, when - Colonel Von der Tann and his German cavalry attack, he will order his men up this street here. When they get to my wall, they will be boxed in; there's no cover, not even a ruddy bathtub to hide in. Remember, we took 'em all.'

He rewards my sincerity with a wry smile.

'Trust me, lad,' I plough on, 'this is going to be a duck shoot.'

Just then, a sniper's bullet zips by my cheek, shatters a yellow-dyed chamber pot in the wall and plops innocently to the dirt.

With a furrowed brow, Jasper thumbs the tip of his shiny bayonet. 'But who'll be the ducks,' he drawls, 'them,' he eyes the iron ball by my foot, daring me to fib, 'or us?'

I brush him off with a chuckle, but his words chew on me, flooding my stomach with acid. He thinks General de Wimpffen's plan is foolhardy and he's spot on; the enemy will crush us; but I must follow orders and so must my men or we risk a blindfold, a shower of bullets and a cosy blanket of French dirt.

The Germans had invaded their unsuspecting neighbour in August of 1870, seemingly hell bent on re-drawing the world map and forcing France to be a member of the tyrannical German Empire. And, so far, the enemy's plan seems to be working perfectly. In only a month of bitter fighting, the German juggernaut has overrun half of France, a plague of

locusts hungry for frogs' legs and French Champagne.

I wonder if Von der Tann, the enemy's heroic colonel, will command the attack on our barricade. Sadly, our 'heroic' French general, de Wimpffen, is a bungling fool. He's led me, my troop of privateers and his army into an inescapable trap, the name of this trap: La Moncelle, a small town in northern France.

And to top it all off, de Wimpffen still thinks he can win.

KAPOOM!

Just up the street, St Barthélemy's chapel blows up in a tempest of flying splinters. Such a sweet church too; I recall the steeple door had a very pretty La Belle Sultane rose carved in it.

I pull a sliver of wood from my shoulder and hunker down with my men. Crooks and murderers the lot of them and I'm no different; they'd pilfer the boots of a bishop, his bible too if they thought it'd sell. Here for the booty, not the shiny medals; but all of them handy with a musket and bayonet. I trust them; I know they will not run till I tell them to.

Relentlessly, the German artillery shells the town. Trees uproot, doors blow up and in. I see a carpenter's hut flip and cartwheel over the roof of the town's school, tidily skewering off two chimney pots and a weather cockerel. I curl up in a ball, my cheeks to my knees. Over and over, tremors jolt my body and booms of thunder ricochet off my skull. I wonder, will the next cannon ball land on me or the man by my elbow.

Finally, the bombardment stops and I look warily up at my wall. To my astonishment, it is still up, chamber pots, bathtubs and all.

I clamber to my feet and, watchful for snipers, I peer over the irreparably chipped top of the cabinet. Most of the Rue de l'Eglise is now lost to a dusty yellow mist, the sun just a milky blob on the horizon, but I spot a cart blazing merrily casting jumping red shadows over the twisted body of a German trooper. My enemy, but still a mother's son. All seems still but for the ever-circling crows and a hangman's noose swinging gently in the breeze - justice for deserters the de Wimpffen way - but I know Von der Tann's cavalry will soon be on us and my fifty-two battle-weary privateers must find a way to stop them.

The cannons were just the warm-up act; a taster, to soften us up.

I feel oddly calm, almost sleepy. I suppose I rely too much on the lucky rabbit's foot in my pocket to ward off the bayonets and bullets. Never been hurt you see; not even a tiny scratch. My men think I'm lucky so they follow me, but I

remember Dad telling me, 'Men who trust in luck need an awful lot of it.' That and, 'Never test the depth of a river with both feet.' I wonder if today is the day my pot of luck finally runs dry.

A pallid-faced corporal trots over and hands me a battered tin mug. He's the new fellow but I remember his name is Pedro; he's from Granada in the south of Spain and by the look of it, he's trying to grow a moustache over his plump goldfish lips. Trying to. 'Orders from General de Wimpffen, Major,' he tells me stiffly. 'He needs to see you. Oh, and he told me to tell you to be prompt. In his words: Now, and not a week on Thursday.'

I thank him for the drink and the news with an even stiffer nod; de Wimpffen is not on my birthday card list. But lifting the coffee to my lips, I spot it ripple ominously.

I cock my head like a wary sparrow, then...

'WAKE UP, LADS!' I yell, dropping the mug in the dirt and snatching up my rifle. 'VISITORS! TWELVE O'CLOCK!'

I rest the barrel of my musket on a bathtub leg, my eyes fixed on the swirling mist. Then, slowly, I thumb back the lock. I'm holding the Enfield rifle-musket, in the chamber a Minié bullet. It has a killing range of over three hundred yards

compared to the fifty yards of the old ball and musket. Invented by Captain Claude Étienne Minié of the French Army; I met him in a bar in Paris a few years ago, cheerful chap, enjoys a spot of rum if I remember correctly - and Cuban cigars.

There is a low rumble. Louder. LOUDER! From the mist gallops the enemy cavalry. A dozen, two, three - hundreds of teeth-baring, eye-bulging troops on teeth-baring, eye-bulging steeds. With swords in fists and howls of 'DRAN! DRAUF! DRÜBER!' they look like devils sent from the pits of hell.

'Hold your fire,' I hiss. An unnecessary warning to my men. They know not to shoot too soon and risk missing. Our muskets may be capable of killing at three hundred yards but only if the musketeer is a remarkably good shot and the target happens to be a barn door or the particularly hefty bottom of a cow. 'Remember, big targets only,' I remind my troopers. 'Go for the chest.'

With the cavalrymen only two hundred feet away, I look up to the early morning sky. The crows circle us keen to enjoy our soft flesh. I hate them. I want to lift my rifle and shoot them but I dare not squander a bullet.

A hundred and fifty feet.

An unstoppable tidal wave of sharpened steel and guts…

A hundred feet.

…snarls and wild eyes, they jump the burning wagon…

Fifty feet.

I jam the butt of my musket to my shoulder. 'FIRE!' I holler.

My name is Tor. Just, Tor. I love crackers with chévre cheese and red wine but only if it's room temperature. I hate turnips, I'm claustrophobic and I'm allergic to cats…

…oh, and I'm a major and a mercenary temporarily in the employ of the French army, my job…to shoot Germans.

0605 hours

Our muskets jump obediently, fifty-two Minié bullets chased by smoke, and grimly I watch the frothing steeds fold. But the regiment of cavalry is brave and deep, the clatter of hoofs seemingly ignorant to our lethal volley.

Unpityingly, they jump the fallen.

I finger my rabbit's foot, my totem. I feel so terribly powerless, driftwood in a raging river. It is like trying to stop a wild bull with a toothpick.

The enemy covers the last twenty feet in seconds, swords

glinting menacingly, keen to find chinks in our cut-price armour.

'FIX BAYONETS!' I bellow, wiping my clammy palms on my tunic.

Time to get dirty.

They assault our make-shift wall; a battering ram of horse muscle, guts and willpower. Frantically, my men and I fire and stab, fire and stab. Everywhere there is blood: my troopers' blood, my enemy's blood, my blood. My bayonet hits bone and snaps off. My luck has finally abandoned me. I'm drowning in screeching men and yells for, 'MOTHER!'

The trooper next to me gets it: a bayonet to the chest. Why him and why not me, I wonder. This is not war, it is a schoolyard scrap. There is no skill to it. If the bullet or the bayonet finds me, it finds me. There is only luck, totally blind, totally wretched luck.

My mind skips to my sister. My poor, poor sister.

Our wall is no longer a wall: the stools crushed, the bathtubs scattered, the French cabinet in tiny jagged splinters.

'FALL BACK!' I cry, snatching up a stool leg and parrying a cavalryman's sword. I hop up on an upturned bathtub and off my back foot I cuff him brutally on the jaw. He yelps and cartwheels off his saddle.

Frantically, I pull my fallen trooper to his feet. It is Gerry, a Londoner; sixteen and never kissed a girl. He is bleeding badly and there is overwhelming terror in his eyes. He will not see the sunset, or kiss a girl, but I throw the poor sod over my shoulder anyway.

Firing our muskets haphazardly, we helter-skelter up the street. We find the doorway to the town's library and scramble through it. There is no roof, no door, no glass in the windows, but a horse cannot follow us in here.

Safe!

For now, anyway.

I lever the injured Gerry to the floor and look around. I count only twenty of us left, cowering in a room of tipped-up desks and burnt and blistered books. I spy a blackened copy of The Three Musketeers, Alexandra Dumas's masterwork of swordplay and honour and the book I most enjoyed when I was a schoolboy.

The clomp of boots. My eyes cut to the doorway. Whispers! German whispers. They must be on foot now. Soon, I know, we will be surrounded and they will overrun us.

General de Wimpffen had promised reinforcements but there is still no sign of them. Murder grips me and I thump the

stool leg on my open palm. The man's a bungling fool.

A shadow by the window.

'Stay low,' I hiss.

Boots crunch.

A German trooper, keen to win a medal, storms our room. He is killed without mercy. I wonder, will his weeping mother get the medal now.

'Major!' An urgent whisper from Jasper. 'Why you holding a stool leg?'

'Oh!' I drop it and pull my sword.

'Brave French troopers!' The words echo in the room. 'This is Colonel Von der Tann of the Seventh German Cavalry. Surrender.'

'He thinks I'm a French ninny,' mutters Jasper. 'How rude.'

I chuckle. 'Very decent of you to surrender so quickly,' I cheekily shout, 'but we'd much prefer to shoot you.'

'Or bayonet you,' my second-in-command adds helpfully.

My men snort and there is the odd jittery chuckle. A nervy thumbs up from Pedro.

Water drips from a cracked gutter ticking off the seconds, and on the floor Gerry looks unblinkingly to the brightening sky. Then, 'So be it, Major Tor.' He says my name slowly, as if tasting the words.

My eyes flicker to Jasper's. 'He knows me,' I mouth. 'How? Why?'

Jasper chews thoughtfully on his thumb. 'Maybe he's a fan or,' he nods knowingly and snaps his fingers, 'he thinks you kissed his sister.'

In an avalanche of howls, they storm the room. Ten, twenty, thirty of them, piling in, all wanting a story to tell to impress a son, a wife, a father. Hand to hand we fight. Dirty, clawing, biting - we fight.

My fight is with the very talented swordsman, Colonel Von der Tann.

The German colonel is lightning fast. I deflect his sword, then off my back foot I lunge but miss, my boots slipping in the rubble. I stumble and my cutlass clanks to the floor. On my knees, I snatch up a book, thrusting it up to protect my eyes. It is the bible, but to the sharpened steel in Von der Tann's fist it is just a soft lump of butter. He runs it through and I look up to find the tip of the colonel's sword only a cat's whisker from the tip of my nose.

Flicking the book away, he drops to a knee and eyes me thoughtfully. I stubbornly return his look. Oddly, I see no thrill there, no joy in his victory over me. He has the cold

eyes of a lizard sunbathing on a rock.

'Colonel!' A call from the street. 'The French!'

The buffoon, de Wimpffen, has sent help at last.

With a scowl, my victor hops to his feet, the news no doubt shadowing his sunny mood. 'GEHEN SIE MÄNNEN!' he howls. 'GEHEN SIE!'

The German cavalrymen scramble over to the door. Then, the colonel eyeballs me, his cutlass unwavering. 'I crossed swords with a gallant man this day,' he tells me in English, bringing up the blade.

Feebly, I pick up my own sword and return the salute. Then I watch him stroll unhurriedly from the room. Why did he not kill me, I wonder.

'MAJOR!' It is Pedro, the corporal with the pubescent caterpillar on his upper lip. 'Jasper's hurt.'

Jumping to my feet, I hurry over. 'STRETCHER PARTY!' I shout, dropping to my knees.

My second-in-command is lying in a corner, his hands clawing at his blood-sodden chest. 'Jesus! Jesus! Jesus!' he is hissing.

'Hold on, lad,' I try to calm him. Roughly, I grip Pedro's tunic. 'Go fetch the ruddy stretcher party.'

'They were all killed.'

I clench my fists. 'BLAST!'

'Forget it, Tor,' Jasper grits his tobacco-rotten teeth and looks to the sky. 'Wretched crows.' His beseeching eyes find me. 'Don't let 'em get me.'

'I won't.'

A tiny drop of blood seeps from his lips. 'Bury me deep, Tor.' He sort of hiccups, spraying me red. 'Hale Mary, f-full of grace, the Lord - the, the Lord...' Then his eyes flutter shut and I'm left in a room of dying men.

Giddy with anger, I jump to my feet. 'Pedro! Hold the fort.'

Startled, the corporal grabs for my torn sleeve, rank forgotten. 'W - why?' he stammers. 'Where y' going?'

'To find a surgeon,' I snarl, wiping Jasper's blood off my cheeks, 'and to pick a fight with de Wimpffen.'

I was born on 25th September, 1844 in Jokkmokk, a tiny town in northern Sweden. My dad is Swedish too but my mum is from Ningbo, a village in China. I blame him for my allergy to cats and her for my dark skin and pond weed eyes: green and grey like an April's day. I love the smell of freshly-mown grass and the hum of insects on a summer's evening...

...oh, and I hate incompetent generals.

0732 hours

After finding a surgeon in the hospital tent and sending him to help my men, and after throwing up over my boots - the smell of blood always turns my stomach - I go and look for de Wimpffen. Not surprisingly, he is skulking in his marquee in the church cemetery. Saluting the sentry, a decent fellow cursed with a club-footed wife, three kids and a lazy sheep dog that pees everywhere, I slip off my iron helmet, duck and march purposefully in.

The French commander, I see, enjoys his comforts. In the corner of the tent there's a bed with a crowning hill of silk pillows, and just by it on a French mahogany desk there sits a bottle of Champagne: a Veuve Clicquot, 1855, a very good year. I spot a six foot candelabra cactus in a pot and on the wall, next to a world map, there is a painting of a leafy forest. A Monet by the look of it; I recognise the clumsy brushwork.

'MAJOR TOR!' A ferrety-eyed man with shiny stars on his shoulders and the soft plumb body of a freshly-baked muffin bobs a stubby finger in my face. 'I can only presume 'prompt' is not in your vocabulary.'

I salute sloppily. 'Sorry, Sir,' I reply in borrowed English. The 'Sir' drips with irony. The man is a fool, a powerful fool.

The most dangerous kind. 'I got held up…'

'Held up!?'

'By the Germans, Sir - you know, the, er - enemy.'

'I KNOW WHO THE ENEMY IS!' he thunders, the medals on his chest jingling merrily.

Eyeing him sceptically, I spot the French Military Medal, Médaille Militaire, and I wonder evilly who he pinched it off.

Colonel Ludovic Fiquet, second-in-command of the French army, throws me a 'Watch it! He's not a happy chappy' scowl from the corner of the tent. Chisel-jawed with a pencil-thin moustache and wire-rimmed specs, he, like me, is no fan of our foolhardy boss. He's also the only trooper I know who can murder me at chess.

I watch General de Wimpffen's left eye twitch, a habit of his. 'I just had terrible news from London. Gladstone, the British prime minister, will not be sending troops to help. So it is up to us.' He thumbs the tip of the riding crop in his ivory-knuckled fist, then, no doubt wishing it was me, or Gladstone, he slaps it on the map on the canvas wall of the tent.

'Just under two hours from now, this is where you and your men must attack, just south of the town.'

My eyes narrow. Uphill, in daylight. He must be mad.

'Destroy the cannons up there,' the general thunders on, 'and maybe we can escape this trap.'

I try to protest. 'But, Sir, if we hold off till sunset…'

'NO!' he barks. 'Every hour of every day the artillery up there murders my men. Frenchmen!' He says the word in such a way to colour my men cannon fodder. 'They must be stopped NOW!'

I nod soberly, swallowing my mutinous thoughts. He's asking the impossible. But then, he's a general and generals often do.

'How many mercs still under your command?' he barks.

A cannon booms and de Wimpffen involuntarily ducks. He's as jumpy as a chicken at a fox's birthday party.

'I prefer the word 'privateer',' I say evenly, 'and there were fifty-two, but Von der Tann's cavalry just attacked and killed most of them.' I swallow, a bristly ball of hurt landing in my stomach with a jolt. 'Now, maybe - ten.'

'Good show.'

My top lip flips up in a snarl. Good. GOOD! I had a hundred and twenty-three men at the start of this bloody war. I finger the hilt of my sword no longer mindful of Fiquet's warning stare.

'On your way, then.' The general is oblivious to my fury. I

step up to him. 'We attack 0930 sharp. Try not to mess it up, Major.'

'WE, Sir?' I can't resist. 'Were you planning to command the attack yourself?'

De Wimpffen scowls. 'Watch it, Trooper.'

Now his other eye is twitching too. I know I should probably back off but annoying pompous fools is my hobby, that, and a not too manly interest in trees and flowers, particularly the juniper and the almond-scented bird cherry. 'Well, Sir, best not to risk it, hey, and it is cosy in here. Tell me, General, all your medals there,' I nod to his chest, 'did you win them on a coconut shy or just whip them off the tunics of dying men?'

'TOR!' Entering the fray, Fiquet darts over and puts a calming hand on my shoulder. 'Stop now, or there'll be hell to pay.'

'No, no, Colonel,' de Wimpffen rests a wobbly buttock on the corner of his desk, 'let Major Tor say what's on his mind.'

I scowl. I'm insulting the idiot, so why is he not ordering his sentry to put me under arrest? Oh well, in for a penny...

'The enemy has over two hundred and twenty thousand troops, out-numbering us almost two to one. From the start of this ridiculous war, he's out-flanked you and out-gunned you.

27

To him, this is a ruddy pheasant shoot.' I feel my blood bubble over, my mood volcanic. 'Your stupidity has led to the death of most of my men.'

De Wimpffen eyes me stonily, seemingly unmoved by my torrent of words. 'You think I'm a coward.'

I glare back mulishly, stiffening my knees. 'No, General, I think you're a fool.'

The seconds tick ponderously by and nobody says a word. I study his piggy eyes and wonder if I will be whipped then shot...

...or simply shot.

Then, to my utmost surprise, he says, 'Jolly good, then. Off you trot. Oh, and good luck.'

Struggling up, he twists on his heels and limps back over to his map. He tells everybody he's got shrapnel in his knee. Pigswill! He's got gout. He's a whisky man; I can tell by his beetroot-red cheeks.

Flabbergasted, I look fleetingly to Fiquet but he just shrugs.

Feeling completely wrong-footed, I forgo the customary salute and march to the door.

'You were born in Sweden, yes?'

Reluctantly, I stop and eyeball de Wimpffen's back. 'Yes.'

Anger burns in my crisp reply.

'Hmm.' He is still studying his map, his index finger on the Swedish city of Stockholm. 'It must be freezing up there.' He grunts. 'Is it?'

'Where you going with this, General?' I snap back.

'If you survive the attack on the hill, there might be a job for you. A different job. Much safer.'

My eyebrows lift. 'A job!?' I muster sceptically.

'The pay will be a lot better,' he shoots me a scornful look over his shoulder, 'and there'll be a lot fewer bullets to dodge.'

Speechless, I scowl and exit the tent. Then, with a wink to the sentry I stop by the flap to listen.

'How's the family?' I whisper.

'Billy's got mumps and the dog peed on the vicar's foot.'

We share a roll of the eyes and a 'Family! Drive y' nuts' look. Which is sort of ironic, for I miss my mum and dad terribly and can never return to them.

'Colonel, go find me a second Swedish trooper,' I hear de Wimpffen bark in French. But I understand him anyway. He's no clue I picked up a little French in Paris a year or so ago. Handy, I find. You never know what the foolish twit will let slip.

'But Tor…' protests Fiquet.

'…will not survive the attack on the hill. Nobody will.'

'So why send him and his men up there?' The colonel's angry tenor retorts. 'It's a fool's errand.'

De Wimpffen grunts mockingly. 'Must I spell it out to you, man? If the rest of his regiment of mercs or privateers or whatever he calls them is wiped out, there will be no need to pay them. Anyway, Tor's a cheeky blighter, calling me a coward…'

'He called you a fool and I'm amazed you let him off so lightly.'

'Let him off! Hardly. But why shoot him with so many Germans keen to do the job for me. He and his men will be massacred, and they will be massacred flying the French flag, my flag. Now, find me a...'

A cannon booms, the general's words lost to the orchestra of war. Grimly, I march off. I will be killed, but fighting for my men and my honour, not for him. I wonder, idly, what the job is and why it is so important for a Swede to do it. Probably too risky for a French trooper. They prefer a chilled bottle of wine to the horrors of war. I however…

Anyway, whatever the jumped-up general has in mind, it has to be safer than spending my days attacking hills swarming with enemy troopers.

It just has to be.

I look old for my twenty-five years, not helped by the silvery curls exploding off my scalp and looping over the four pips on my collar. The cleft on my chin is ugly but the dimple in my cheek is, according to my mum, 'adorable'. My Adam's apple, however, is not. I suspect, when I was a baby I swallowed a conker and now it's just stuck there. Bullish shoulders, angular jaw; children run away when they see me.

Better that way.

0909 hours

I jump up on my horse, Ushry, a trusty fellow who's been with me for years. Then I trot off to find my men.

The town looks truly awful, the result of two weeks of relentless cannon fire. I'm almost hypnotised by the hills of splintered bricks and watery craters. The Town Hall, I see, no longer has a roof, blackened timbers poking up over the tops of the walls, enjoying the sun. A scattered chunk of chimney pot attempts to skewer Ushry's hoof and he must hop over a mangled weather cockerel and then the trunk of a maple tree.

I see it has been ripped up by the roots. I suck in my cheeks, a gloomy melancholy washing over me. It probably took a hundred years to grow and only a tenth of a second to destroy.

I find my men over by the town well, mounted up and, seemingly, all set to go.

'Ok, lads,' I shout; the wind is howling, whipping up the dust and turning our skins pink, 'you know the drill. Our job's to destroy the artillery on the hill over there.'

Embarrassed by what I must order them to do, I nod to the hill and the cluster of German cannons sitting smugly on top of it. I can tell instantly what every man in my company is thinking. For I happen to be thinking it too. Between us and the enemy there is only a tiny river, a pond with the odd wind-bent bulrush in it and a patch of buttercups. Hardly a tree; hardly a bush. In fact, hardly any cover at all.

'We'll be blown to smithereens,' grunts Pedro, stroking the flapping mane of his horse.

'Perhaps,' I admit, 'but the French army's trapped and the cannons up there will very soon destroy what's left of it. Keep in mind, this is what the French pay us to do.'

'How they going to pay Jasper?' mutters the corporal.

I can think of no answer to this so I try to shut him up with a frosty look and a deep furrow of my brow.

'Why us?' protests Alejandro bitterly. He is from Florence in Italy and always has on cowboy boots, spurs and all. 'Why not the French cavalry?'

'Orders,' I snap back, 'and anybody disobeying them will face a French bullet.' I'm keen for my men to focus on the job.

'Orders!' bursts out Pedro. Our timid corporal is no longer so timid. What war will do to a man. 'From ruddy de Wimpffen, I bet.' He spits a lump of tobacco in the dirt. 'He's a dimwit and a coward - and his orders stink.'

I nod. 'Yes, they do and he is, but we signed up for this party, so stop your bellyaching, say your prayers and let's do this.' I wave a balled-up fist at them. 'Remember boys, we do this for honour, for...'

BOOM!

The crash of artillery interrupts my 'rally the troops' speech. Not to worry; it was ruddy terrible anyway. My stomach's just not in it. In fact, a few of the men had begun to trot off.

I look up to see the French cannons bombarding the hill. With any luck the German gunners will find cover in bunkers till the bombing stops and not spot our crazy attack.

'Giddy up!' I kick my heels and gallop off, my men

following me.

With any luck.

0930 hours

We hit the hill.

Feverishly, I urge Ushry on. I risk a glance over my shoulder and spy ten snarling privateers in my dust. Any doubts I had melt away and I signal for them not to bunch up. That way, they will be a lot harder to hit. I hope.

Two hundred yards away, up on the hill, French cannon balls keep the enemy's cheeks flattened to the cold dirt.

General de Wimpffen's plan seems to be working.

I see a tree topple, geysers of mud and rocks exploding up in the sky. A German cannon belly flops to the dirt, another flips, the wheels shattering into hundreds of flying splinters.

Abruptly, the French bombardment stops. Too early, I think in fury. TOO EARLY! Blast de Wimpffen to hell.

I can see the enemy's guns better now and to my horror, the German gunners sprinting over to them. A split second later, I watch the barrels slowly lower, keen to put us in our tombs.

'FASTER!' I yell to Ushry, yanking my sword from my belt.

KAPOOM!

Two of my troopers blown to the wind.

KAPOOM!

A wall of flying rocks and dirt; my Spanish corporal, Pedro, cartwheels to his doom.

Almost on the vermin now. Almost. ALMOST!

I thunder down on the first of the cannons and slash wildly at the cowering Germans. My sword finds the chest of a major and, coldly, I watch him crumple to his knees.

In his wild, darting eyes I see the devil; a horrifying monster with a thorny hallow of brutality.

But it is me; his eyes simply a mirror.

The rest of the artillerymen try to outrun my chopping sword, but with the mercy they showed my torn and bloody troopers, I do the devil's work and send them off to hell.

Up on the very top of the hill, in a copse of birch trees, a cannon I had not spotted opens up. It is as if a volcano has erupted, my world suddenly a jumbled nightmare of screeching cannon balls and screeching men.

A tidal wave of flying rocks hits me and it is Ushry's and

my turn to tumble to the dirt. My left cheek burns, hot sticky blood filling my mouth, choking me. I try to sit up but my foot is trapped under the saddle.

The mongrels murdered my horse.

So I just lay there, watching the rest of my company of men being butchered.

By my cheek I spy a Lady's mantle, a very clever little plant, the leaf cup-shaped to catch the morning dew. I very gently touch the lime-tinted petals. They feel so soft, so silky... 'Flowers grow out of the darkest moments,' I murmur.

Finally. Thankfully. The booms stop. Only then can I shut my eyes to this hilltop abattoir and meet my demons.

0930 hours, The King's Castle, Stockholm, Sweden

She sits on the cold floor, the worn blanket she slept on by her feet. The cellar is freezing and damp and smells strongly of mildew; even the rats look cold, cuddled up in a corner in a whiskery lump of grey patchy fur.

Footsteps! Clomping boots on tired old wood. Terror fills her.

A key is turned and the door hits the wall with a dull thud.

'Get up!' yells the man. He is bow-shouldered with dangly gorilla limbs and a soft buttery chin. 'Run to the scullery,' he tells her austerely. 'Help the butlers to polish the silver; then the floor in there must be swept. Properly,' he adds with a sneer.

She attempts to scramble past him, her anklets of silver bells jingling merrily. But his fist finds her temple. She trips and falls to her knees, nursing her reddened cheek.

'The king's birthday party is in eighteen days and there is much to do.'

'Y-yes, Father,' she stutters, stifling a sob. She has the red eyes of an injured dog that has no idea why her master is angry with her.

'Then, GO!'

She jumps ups and runs for it, his cruel laugh chasing her scampering feet.

Wednesday, 2nd September, 1870
17 Days to Assassination Day

0937 hours, Hospital Tent, La Moncelle

In a whirl of terror, but knowing I must, I feel my way out from my cosy blanket of sleep to find the welcoming frown of Colonel Ludovic Fiquet.

'If y' God's angel,' I mutter groggily, 'I think I prefer the joys of hell.'

He titters in a boyish sort of way. 'Don't worry, Tor. If I dabbled in poker, I'd bet my family's vineyard on hell for you, probably just by the devil's elbow.' He sobers and the smile drops off his lips. 'So, how do you feel, Trooper?'

Gingerly, I press my fingers to my throbbing cheek but it is wrapped in a wad of padded cloth. 'Skewered,' I croak. It hurts to talk and I wonder if, when I fell, did I accidentally swallow a prickly cactus.

'You were, and er, pretty badly,' he adds. He thumps me playfully on the shoulder. 'Hey! Chin up. Everybody knows women worship men with scars.'

I thank him for his show of joviality with a tiny curl of my

lips. Sadly, he is not the most accomplished of actors, his words a little hollow, his smile a little too statuesque.

With a little help from the colonel, I slowly sit up in my bed. To my stomach-churning horror, I find I'm in the hospital tent. Everywhere, troopers lay in hammocks, doctors rushing here, there and everywhere in a frenzy of probing, injecting and sawing.

I look to my legs.

'Still there,' murmurs Fiquet gently.

I nod and swallow. The stink is horrific: the sweet, metallic smell of blood mixed with rotting pork; a butchers' market on a hot day, and there is a constant whimpering broken only by the odd intermittent soul-destroying cry.

I am in hell. Thankfully, my stomach's so empty I can't throw up.

'My men?' I know the answer; it is festering in my gut, but I must ask.

The colonel looks to his dust-lacquered boots. 'Sorry.'

'Not all of them,' I choke. I feel so numb I wonder how I can possibly exist.

'Yes, but for you. You were lucky. A stretcher party stumbled over your horse.'

It is a terribly bitter pill to swallow and I tightly shut my eyes. Luck. Blind wretched luck. Desperately, I hunt my pockets for my rabbit's foot. I find it and squeeze it in my fist. I feel I'm swimming in a river of hurt. A river I remember all too well. My sister. My sweet little...

'Tor.'

I'm drowning. DROWNING!

I squeeze even harder.

'TOR!'

I blink open my eyes. Through my fog of self pity, I watch Fiquet pull up a stool and sit. 'De Wimpffen still needs you to do this job.'

I frown and rub my damp eyes, trying to remember.

'It seems our beloved general is in debt to the Crown Prince of Denmark. They play poker and trust me, de Wimpffen's pretty awful. Anyway, this prince needs a job doing and he needs a Swedish trooper to do it,' he flips me a wink, 'and you happen to be the only Swede in the French army. I know, he had me look. Go to Copenhagen.' He puts a scroll by my feet. 'Here're your orders; they will get you by the palace sentry.'

I grunt. Copenhagen is the capital city of Denmark and only a ferry hop from Sweden, my home. 'But will they get me by the army camped on our doorstep?' I challenge him.

41

'De Wimpffen plans to attack the village of Floing at 1400. During the battle, you must escape to Calais.'

'CALAIS!' I explode, my cut cheek protesting almost as angrily. 'That must be a two day ride.' Then, sullenly, I chunter, 'I will be lucky if I can even climb on a horse.'

'You will find a ship docked there called the Flying Spur,' the colonel ploughs on unperturbed. 'A yacht of sorts. The crew has been ordered to carry you to Copenhagen.'

Reluctantly, I nod. Why not? I'm a criminal on the run, cut off from my family, my men massacred. I can do this or put a bullet in my skull.

But out of the frying pan, into the - what, I wonder.

Fiquet's lips curl up. 'Good news: De Wimpffen has been ordered to command the attack on Floing.'

Justice, at last.

'The old windbag must be over the moon,' I chuckle, feeling wonderfully spiteful. It is astonishing how another man's misfortune can improve a fellow's mood. 'Tell me, is he planning to bring his Monet and six foot cactus with him?'

But the colonel interrupts my jesting by candidly telling me, 'I will be going with him.'

The smile slips from my lips. 'You will be killed,' I say matter-of-factly.

'Yes,' he shrugs his bony shoulders, 'I know.' Digging in his tunic pocket he hands me a slim envelope. 'A letter for my mother in Aytré in southern France. I lost my father to cancer and I'm her only child, no bothers, no sisters; so there'll be nobody left but her. But it's better she knows. I don't want her to spend the rest of her life watching the door.'

I nod soberly. 'You can rely on me.'

'I know I can.' He props a thin smile on his lips and stands up. 'Good luck, Major - oh, and de Wimpffen told me this Prince Frederick, or whatever his name is, is a sly fox and tricky as a box of monkeys, so don't trust him.'

'In this game, I don't trust anybody.'

Crinkling his brow, he nods. Then he offers me his hand. 'Adieu.'

I shake it. 'Goodbye.'

With sadness, I watch the brave Colonel Ludovic Fiquet march from the tent. I will miss his cheerful ways. Gingerly, I sit up and put my feet on the floor.

'Get back to bed,' a nurse shouts, scurrying over. She has the looks, hips and empathy of a bull hippo; sadly, no Florence Nightingale. 'You must sleep,' she tells me firmly.

'I can sleep when a bayonet finds me,' I snap back, which undoubtedly will be very, very soon.

43

I stagger drunkenly from the tent. I must return to the burnt-out library, find Jasper's body, Gerry's too, and bury them; bury them deep. Then I must collect my pay from the quartermaster's tent and find a speedy horse.

1350 hours

I stand by a drooping willow tree on the outskirts of La Moncelle and watch the remnants of the French army trot by. They look a sorry mess: red tunics in tatters, boots thick with mud; a pitiful band of hollow-eyed troopers on stooped-over mounts. The foolishly fat General de Wimpffen trots past, on his shoulder, Colonel Fiquet. I salute but only the colonel bothers to return it. De Wimpffen is too busy trying to stop his horse from bolting. I smirk; I had a hand in that. I can see the panic in the French commander's eyes and it is not just his bucking horse. I suspect he's missing his cosy marquee.

I drop to a knee to gently finger the petals of a St. Bernard's lily, in Latin, Anthericum ramosun. My mum is a lover of flowers so I had grown up loving them too. She always told me to trust them. 'Not even a king can challenge the ideology of a rose,' she always insisted.

However, my dad, the skipper of a cotton ship and a connoisseur of moonshine and belching, is mostly a carrot and spud man.

I march over to the burnt timbers of a barn to collect the horse I had stolen and hidden there. I did not want de Wimpffen to see him. He's his horse! Jumping up on the spirited fellow, I follow the French cavalrymen's winding tail to the outskirts of Floing village. There I swing left and climb a hill.

From up here, I can easily see Floing: a tiny cluster of greyish bricks, thatched roofs and smoking chimneys. I spy a church too, the steeple tidily decapitated by a random cannon ball.

There is a war cry from the village and the German cavalry trots out to meet the French; hundreds of them, a swarm of bees, rod-backed, uniforms glossy blue. I reckon they must outnumber the French three to two.

I watch de Wimpffen swing his sword and with banners flying they attack the oncoming cavalry. He is braver than I thought.

But suddenly, with only two hundred yards to go, the general pulls up his horse and gallops away, back to La Moncelle.

The cowardly devil is deserting his men.

I jump off my horse and pull my rifle from the saddle holster. Squatting, I rest the barrel on my palm and my elbows on my knees. Then I thumb back the lock and relax my index finger ever so gently on the trigger.

It looks to be two hundred and fifty, maybe two hundred and sixty yards; a difficult shot for most, but not for me. The clever fingers of a London gunsmith had seen to that. Not only had he lengthened the barrel of my musket by almost a foot, he had also developed a scope, a new way of magnifying a target so now I can hit a prancing rabbit at almost half a mile. A sneer shadows my lips. De Wimpffen's hefty chest presents no problem whatsoever.

I look to the trees. The wind is blowing from the west, ten, maybe fifteen knots. I sight my rifle a foot or so in front of the fleeing general and slowly caress the trigger.

Suddenly, de Wimpffen throws up his hands, slipping off his saddle. His foot gets trapped in the stirrup and he is dragged by his horse through the dirt.

But I did not shoot!

Lowering my musket, I quickly spot Fiquet and the smoking pistol in his fist. The colonel has beaten me to it. I watch him throw the gun away, draw his sword and with a

46

howl, attack the oncoming cavalrymen.

I blow out my cheeks. If I was a man of the church, I'd remember him in my prayers. Sadly, I'm not. Not now, anyway.

Unexpectantly, the left flank of the enemy veers off and gallops my way.

'Not good,' I murmur. 'NOT GOOD!' Holstering my rifle, I jump up on my horse and kick him savagely. 'GO! GO! GO!' I yell and away we speed.

It seems it is I who needs a prayer now.

Thursday, 3rd September, 1870
16 Days to Assassination Day

1425 hours, 1 mile south of St. Omer, France

I ride through the night, passing through the tiny village of Lens and over the Canal D'Aire, the Germans relentlessly on my heels. My new horse is a lipizzano, from Italy, a wonderfully spirited breed and dogged to boot but even he cannot gallop forever. But nor can the enemy in my dust, so,

when they walk, we walk, when they trot, we trot, when they stop for food (dry pork and cold coffee), so do we. I try to keep three hundred yards between them and us, too far to shoot, but it is exhausting; a gnawing, grinding war.

Thankfully, we travel further into France and away from the invading Germans. To begin with there had been twenty or so of the blighters, but now, so far from the safety of the rest of the German army, many of them melt away.

Now there is only a handful left, but a very determined handful. I frown, wondering why they want to catch me so badly.

We battle up a hill, the westerly wind whipping in our eyes, slowing us to a crawl. I shoot a look over my shoulder and I spot my hunters by a cluster of tree stumps. They seem much closer now and, suddenly, a bullet shrills by my cheek, ricocheting off a rock.

I spy a small wood and with an urgent kick of my heels, we gallop over to it. There, I jump off, pulling my horse away from the path and in amongst the trees. Grabbing my rifle, I hide in ambush by a very old chestnut tree. The trunk is scorched; hit by lightning perhaps.

The thump of hoofs in the dirt.

Ever so slowly, I rest my musket's long barrel on a fallen

branch and work on my breathing: in through the nose, out through the mouth. I relax my shoulders and try to empty my mind of Jasper, Pedro and the rest of my murdered men. I see the riders and gently, very gently, I caress the trigger.

BOOM! A deer bolts, a swarm of birds fly up from the chestnut and a cavalryman drops with a yelp to the path.

With howls of surprise, the rest of them jump off and run for cover, ducking in amongst the greenery.

The trick is to fire and crawl, fire and crawl; the enemy will soon think he's fighting a shadow. Sadly, I possess the agility and unfettered grace of a baby with a bucket of bricks. With bullets whizzing over me, I drop to my belly and shuffle over to a nettle patch. A branch snaps; I kick over a rock. Then, ignoring the stings, I nestle down in it.

I may be no hotshot swordsman, but I'm the best musketeer in the French army. I just hope I'm the best in the German army too. Urgently, I empty gunpowder from my powder horn into the muzzle of my musket, followed by a Minié bullet. After jamming them up it with the ramrod, I cock the rifle by clicking back the lock.

I stay perfectly still. Watching, forever watching. I spot the yellow petals of a wild chrysanthemum and a butterfly, a sooty copper I think, sunning her polkerdot wings on the

trunk of a eucalyptus tree. My eyes find an O'Kelly's orchid, or, in Latin, the Dactylorhiza fuchcii. Such a pretty flower, a clump of ivory-white buds atop a sturdy stem. If only I had my pen with me but, typically, it's in my saddle. I risk a look over my shoulder. Thankfully, my horse is still there. I hope they will not think to shoot him; if they do, I'm finished.

A branch snaps.

Over to my left.

Slowly, I swing my rifle, my eyes on a trembling gorse bush. I spot a trooper peering over the top…

BOOM!

He grabs for his chest and falls to the leafy forest floor.

I drop low and, on all fours, scamper away. A second later the nettle patch I had been hiding in is smattered with bullets.

This is crazy. There is no way I can stop all six of them. I know most cavalrymen take thirty-five seconds to fill a musket with powder and ball, so I scramble to my feet and dash over to my horse.

Thirty seconds.

I hop up on a rock, jump and land crookedly in the saddle.

Twenty-five seconds.

'Giddy up!' A brutal kick and we sprint for the path.

Twenty seconds.

A branch thumps my cheek, ripping off the bandage.

Ten seconds.

The urgent yells of my enemy.

BOOM! They did it much quicker than I had thought.

I gallop up the path, zinging bullets kicking up the dirt and hammering the tree trunks. Only four of them left, I think grimly. The odds have gotten better.

I see curling smoke in the distance; it must be a village. I shoot a look over my shoulder. My enemy is only twenty yards away looking grim and determined in my dust. I jump a fallen log and then clatter over a bridge, disturbing a family of otters enjoying a salmon lunch. My cheek is in agony, but racing up a hill I still keep it pressed firmly to the clammy neck of my horse.

We turn a corner and there's the village, St. Omer branded on the gnarled trunk of an apple tree just by the path.

It is market day and the French village is packed with haggling traders, gossiping old women and barking dogs. Clattering over the cobbled square, I pull up my horse and stubbornly turn to face my hunters.

They stop too. To my astonishment, I see Von der Tann. If he is here, who is running hell, I wonder. He is eyeing me suspiciously, but I can tell what he's thinking: Why is the

major not running? Is it a trap?

With stiff backs and hands on swords, they clip clop through the crowd. They stop only six feet short of me.

'Major Tor,' growls Von der Tann in a deep, musical base, snapping off a bow. He looks very dapper in a blue tunic buttoned up to the collar and riding boots laced up to the knees. His jaw is hard and angular and a trimmed sandy-blond moustache sits on his bloodless lips. He has the sort of devilishly chiselled face I always wish would look back at me from a mirror.

'Colonel.' I nod formally, putting up my hands in mock surrender.

'You're a long way from the war,' he says slowly. 'Trying to escape, perhaps?' His eyes dart here and there like a mouse trying to watch too many cats.

I shrug. 'No, it was the French grub; the frogs legs. I get terrible wind.'

He rewards my joviality with the ghost of a smile. 'Deserting your men. How very dishonourable of you.'

'You murdered all my men,' I snap off.

'No, your foolish de Wimpffen murdered all your men.'

Onlookers gather, trying to comprehend our broken English words.

'Why did you not kill me in the library?' I bluntly put to him. 'You bettered me.'

De Tann cocks his eyebrow. 'You were just unlucky. You slipped in the rubble; dropped your sword. I never kill in cold blood.' He eyes me curiously, no doubt hoping to unlock my secrets. 'Mercenary, yes…?'

'I prefer 'privateer',' I interrupt him. I know I'm being a little rude but he probably plans to kill me and, in my book, that's considerably ruder.

He nods and smirks. 'We need good troopers. We pay well too; better than the French. Plus, if you work for me, you will live to spend it.'

I answer him by yelling, 'ALLEMANDES!' The French word for 'GERMANS!'

The crowd stops: the market traders stop haggling, the old women stop gossiping, even the dogs stop barking. The bakers stop baking and the butchers stop butchering. They look to me and my waggling finger and quickly, an angry mob gathers.

I admit, not the most gentlemanly way to fight, but then nor is four on one, and with a mocking salute I gallop off.

I feel Von der Tann's eyes still on me. I shoot a look over my shoulder but my hunter is lost in a thrashing pool of jeers

and flying fists.

Friday, 4th September, 1870
15 Days to Assassination Day

1935 hours, The Port of Calais, France

It is drizzling and almost dark when I finally see the outskirts of Calais. I trot over a low hill and there it is: hundreds of burning lanterns and the sweet smell of the salty water.

I trot down the hill to the town. My horse needs a rest, so tiredly I clamber off him and walk. My cheek is torturing me, and to add to my misery there is a damp gusty wind blowing in off the English Channel.

The port of Calais is a melting pot of rats, cats and scallywags. Nobody here will meet my eye. With collars turned up and hats pulled down, the good citizens of the town tramp by me, cursing the mud and giving off a sinister aura of being 'up to no good'.

I clump by the rotten shutters of a shop, a fishmongers by the smell of it, and a man sprawled on his bottom in a shadowy corner trying to tempt me over with whispers of 'free booze'. No doubt his chum is hidden in the shadows too, his job to knock me out so they can pilfer my wallet and boots.

I spy a café brimming with rowdy drinkers and I'm tempted to pop in for a hot bowl of mushroom soup and a shot of rum. I'm surprised it is so busy. It's odd; they do not seem to worry the German army is only ten days march away.

Eventually, I get to the docks. It is ringed by a wall, spiked on the top, but I spot the barbed roof of a sentry's hut.

I pull my horse over to it.

'Dock's shut,' calls a well-fed sentry, swaggering over to me. He has the melancholy look of a paddocked donkey.

I nod. 'I'm looking for a ship, a yacht called the Flying Spur.'

'Listen 'ere mate,' his hand drops to the hilt of his sword, 'I'm not interested. Even if you're looking for a lost puppy for a crying kid, I'm not interested. You see, today's Friday and the dock's just shut for the weekend, end of story.'

My nostrils flare. 'I've got orders,' I counter sharply.

Chewing on his gums, he snaps his stubby fingers. 'Let's see 'em, then.'

Reluctantly, I hand him the scroll and watch with interest

the drop of his jaw and the widening of his eyes. Hastily, he hands it back to me. 'Dock Seven,' he mutters, sending me on my way. I had not bothered to look at the orders, but I do now: signed by de Wimpffen himself. No wonder the sentry's eyes had almost popped from their sockets.

The dock, I find, is not just a dock, it is a junkyard. A junkyard full of traps: old rusty anchors and steel fish hooks trying to trip me up and wonky pyramids of wicker baskets tilting dangerously, keen to bury me.

We clip clop by a gallant Man of War, her cannon ports shut for the night, and a crate lashed to an old rusted winch, COFFEE branded in the wood. I spot the bottom corner's been ripped off and coffee has spilt over the dock's mildewed planks.

Suddenly, out of the ghostly shadows, steps Von der Tann. His tunic, I see, is torn and there is a nasty gash in his chin. How the hell did he find me, I wonder.

In a flash, I pull my sword from my scabbard. 'Nasty cut,' I say blithely.

He shoots me such a wintry smile, I actually feel cold. 'I had a spot of bother with the French villagers. Clever, by the way, but hardly,' he frowns, 'what's the name of that English sport, you know, where they dress up in jumpers and try to knock over three wooden…'

'Cricket,' I interrupt him helpfully, 'and war is not a sport.'

In a flurry of powdery sparks, he attacks, our swords click-clicking like steel-capped boots on scurrying mice. I try to parry but he twirls his wrist and a tuft of my curls drifts to the dock floor.

I swallow. He is much better, faster too, with a hint of 'look at me' flamboyance.

But I know how to play dirty.

I drop to a knee, snatch up a fistful of spilt coffee beans and hurl them in his eyes. A boot to the knee, a fist to the jaw and he drops.

Tor wins! Well, it happens. Not too frequently, I admit. But it happens.

I press the tip of my cutlass to his cut chin. 'Why did you follow me all the way here?' I demand of my prisoner.

'Orders.' He spits blood on my boot.

'Orders!' I frown. 'Who from?'

'I cannot tell you. If I do, he will murder me.'

'Who? Who will murder you?'

He shows me his palms, pursing his lips stubbornly, so I wallop him with the hilt of my sword, knocking him out.

Now what shall I do with him? If he is discovered, the

French will think he's a spy and he will be shot. A brave man merits better. Even a brave German. And, anyway, he did show me mercy when I slipped and fell over in the library. So I drag him over to a nest of corn sacks and hide him there.

Scowling, I holster my sword. My mind is a jumble, the thump in my chest lopsided like a one-man band. A colonel in the German army chasing a lowly mercenary all the way through France! Why?

I can see Dock Seven from here and the blurry phantom of what must be the Flying Spur. A hundred feet from bow to stern, the lantern on her tallest mast casts a creepy yellow sheen over her abandoned deck and the limpets and mussels on her dented hull. A clipper by the look of the tapered stern; and a bit of a relic. If she was a mule, she'd be blind with a limp.

Bow-shouldered, I collect my horse and we clip-clop over to her.

Saturday, 5th September, 1870

14 Days to Assassination Day

0645 hours, The English Channel

I stand on the bow of the Flying Spur watching the French towns and hamlets pass us by. It is the next morning and the feeble autumn sun has crept up on the horizon with the gusto of a turkey waking up on Christmas day.

I just enjoyed a dish of scrambled egg and bacon courtesy of the ship's Japanese cook and I'm feeling much better. Even my horse seems happy; he is below deck enjoying a bucket of oats and a rest. He is a good horse, fast too, so I decide to call him Blixt, Swedish for lightning.

I warm my hands on my mug of coffee and idly watch the ship's cat, Prissy, try pitifully to catch the gulls on the deck. My mind is still a jumbled mess: the men I lost, Fiquet's letter to his mother burning a hole in my pocket, but mostly Von der Tann. Why was it so important to him to stop me? Had he been told of my job for the Danish prince and, if he had, who had told him? I wonder too how he had known where to find me: on Dock Seven by the Flying Spur.

So many unknowns. Mentally, I pop them in a box and shift them to a cobwebby corner in the back of my skull.

The cut on my cheek is still throbbing merrily away but, thankfully, the cook helped me to dress it. I, in turn, took the opportunity to quiz him about the ship. It seems I was correct and the Flying Spur is a clipper, her usual job to cart tea to and from China. But the skipper, a chap called Church, and his crew, Compass Cob, Oddjob and the chef, had been offered a wad of cash to pick me up and whisk me off to Copenhagen.

The cook is a chatty sort of fellow and his English is surprisingly fluent. He even told me where he got the cool tattoo of the spider on his wrist: not Tokyo but London, a tiny shop on Joy Street, a stone's throw away from Big Ben. The cook, it seems, is a well-travelled man.

I swallow the last of my coffee and rest the tin mug on the wooden deck.

The Flying Spur is looking a tad shabby, from the rotten fishing nets draped over the stern (undoubtedly for catching the crew's supper) to the barnacle-encrusted anchor by my feet. Even the stuffed swordfish on the outer cabin wall is hanging crookedly. Nevertheless, she's a sprightly lady, from the top of her thirty foot middle mast to the smooth cut of her bow.

The Japanese cook strolls over to me with a pot of coffee. I grab up my mug. 'You're a life saver,' I tell him, which is sort of funny considering he is planning to murder me.

He drops the pot and kicks me so hard in the chest he almost knocks me to my knees. I throw my mug at him and swing my fist but he is too fast, so fast I can no longer see his hands and feet, but I feel them, in my eye, my jaw, my poor knee.

It seems the ship's cook is a Kong fu expert.

With a jackal's cry, he jumps up, but with his heel only a whisker from my chin, I block it and punch him in the belly. He reels back, his eyebrows arched. Perhaps the wolf did not expect the lamb to show his teeth.

With fists flying, he lumbers back over to me, but I duck, drop low and sweep my foot. Nimbly, he hops over it.

Now it is his turn.

He thumps me; an uppercut to the jaw. Then he twists and flips me over his shoulder, cartwheeling me to the floor. I clamber drunkenly to my feet but a hammering fist wallops me on the cleft of my chin, cracking my teeth. I lurch back, hitting the cabin wall. Blurry-eyed, I watch him march up to me, murder glinting in his almond-shaped eyes.

'STOP!' I cry. 'This is crazy.' But he is on me like a fat boy on a muffin.

Desperately, I grab for the swordfish, ripping it off the wall and with a cry of anger, I plunge it into his chest.

Yelping in agony, the cook staggers away from me. 'You will feel the sting of Wasp for this,' he yells cryptically. In horror, I watch him topple off the deck, landing in the water with a tremendous splash.

'No coffee for me, then,' I murmur. Still in shock, I spit a splinter of tooth to the deck.

Church, the ship's skipper, runs over. He is small and tubby with a sloppy crew-cut and red welty skin. Perhaps he's allergic to cats too.

'You killed the cook,' he bellows at me, 'and lost me my prize swordfish. I hooked him off Italy; took me two bleedin' hours to reel him in.'

I frown. The cook or the swordfish, I wonder. But I can tell he's upset.

Collapsing to the deck, I rally up a tiny nod. 'If it's any help, I cook very good spaghetti,' I tell him jadedly.

The cat smirks at me, licking his paws. Then I spot blood on my cuff. My blood! And, promptly, I throw up over the skipper's left boot. This cheers him up considerably.

2318 hours, Bernadotte Library, The King's Castle, Stockholm, Sweden

Gurli sits on the floor of the Bernadotte Library, her back to a grandfather clock, books towering over her. It is not so comfortable and the lump over her eye throbs mercilessly, but she is too engrossed in Alfred Nobel's scientific tome to worry.

She is kneeling by the window but the moon and the clouds seem unwilling to form a truce this night. Thankfully, the candle by her foot is helping her to decipher the scribbled equations and the labels on the diagrams.

She has just got to Chapter Seven and the Swedish inventor is describing the inner-workings of nitro-glycerine.

With the intensity of a nun saying her vows, she gulps down the words. To Gurli, every paragraph is a voyage of discovery, every sentence, every word a stepping stone to knowledge.

There is a thump and she looks up, her belly tightening in fright. A chill creeps up from the bottom of her feet, up through her heels to the roots of her curls. She is not supposed to be in here. If they catch her, her father will do what he

always did to punish her: unbuckle his belt.

The pendulum in the clock tick tocks pompously back and forth and, slowly, she drops her eyes to the book.

The library is her cave, her sanctuary, her only escape.

Monday, 7th September, 1870
12 Days to Assassination Day

1426 hours, Copenhagen, Denmark

Two days on the Flying Spur and we get to Copenhagen. It has been a stormy trip and I spent most of the voyage trying not to vomit, trying to cook food for the crew, and trying not to vomit in the crew's food. I always enjoy being in the kitchen so on the second day I rustled up a very tasty spaghetti and on the third a superb cherry-topped apple crumble.

I quizzed Skipper Church on my attacker but the chef had been new. He had been taken on in Shanghai on the last trip to China; a bum, a waster who had needed a job.

I wonder now what the Japanese cook had even been doing

in China.

Church had then offered me the job of ship's cook. It seems he enjoyed my spaghetti. That or he thinks I'm a waster too. I had declined with an apologetic smile. I then went on to recommend he put tannin on his fishing nets. 'You can find it in the quebracho tree,' I had told him. 'It will help to keep the rope soft.'

When I disembark in Copenhagen, I'm astonished to be met by three of the Danish monarch's troops. It seems I'm a Very Important Person. I show them de Wimpffen's orders and instantly they bundle me on a wagon and whisk me off to Denmark's Royal Palace.

A dusty, rickety half hour later, I'm stood in the throne room trying not to scratch. On my second day on the Flying Spur I had awoken to find Prissy, the ship's cat, curled up on my chest. Courtesy of my allergy, it is now a chest carpeted in red welts. If I was a little tubby too, I'd be Skipper Church's twin.

It is a wonder to see such a splendid room, the row upon row of perfectly arched windows, the cherrywood floors buffed to mirrors and the ornate-framed monarchs peering snootily down on me from rose-pink, pattern-papered walls. A slim red carpet splits the room in two from the door all the

way up to the throne. I see it rests on a splendidly handsome tiled box so even when the king is sitting he is still the tallest in the room.

Wandering over to the arched windows, I discover a magnificent garden of grassy daisy-rich hills and pink-petalled flower beds. I spy a blood trumpet, a yellow shower tree, even the buds of a Chinese cracker flower, my Grandmother Toyi's favourite. The flowers always remind me of tiny partly-peeled bananas.

I frown and my eyes narrow. Is that a…?

'Wonderful, is it not?'

I twist on my heels to find Prince Frederick of Denmark marching over to me, a wolf by his heels. I can tell it is the prince. The king must be older and, anyway, I can always tell royalty; most of them look so stiff, if they bent over they'd probably snap in half.

'This palace was built by the last Swedish king, Karl XlV Johan,' he tells me. His English is almost perfect; his vowels just a little sharp perhaps. 'The gardens too with flowers shipped in from all over the world. A present to poor Denmark from our filthy rich neighbour.'

'My Prince.' I bow, my eyes drawn to the glimmering sword on his belt.

The wolf jumps up on the throne and curls in a ball. He is a monster of a dog, his fur ivory-white, his paws peppered black. I hop uncomfortably from foot to foot. His yellow eyes rest on me in such a way I begin to feel a little like a lamb casserole.

'This is my pet wolf, Skufsi Tennur,' Frederick tells me blankly. 'He's from Iceland.'

I frown. Odd name for a pet. But, then, it's a very odd pet. The wolf says hello with a fang-filled snarl.

'How, er, sweet,' I stammer, shuffling slightly back. He is sort of bony and I spot a gooey welt on his hindquarters. He must be old.

'So, de Wimpffen sent you, did he?'

I nod.

'Kan du prata Svenska?'

'Ja,' I respond in Swedish. 'I was born in Jokkmokk so my Swedish is excellent.'

'Good.' He eyes me sternly. He knows how to shout with those eyes.

The prince is tall and slender with thin lips the colour of an old penny and perfectly trimmed eyebrows. There is a sort of waxy polish to his skin and surprisingly, for a man of only twenty-seven, he has crow's feet fanning out from the corners of his murky brown eyes. He has on a ruby-red velvet tunic with silk cuffs and a gold-buckled belt, and a yellow sash connects his shoulder to his hip.

He smells of lavender.

'General de Wimpffen was killed by the way,' I tell him bluntly.

'He was, was he? Blast! The old blighter owed me a fortune in gold. Terrible poker player, old de Wimpffen, which I guess is why you're here.'

I nod, wordlessly. Colonel Fiquet had been spot on. The French general had sent me to pay off his gambling debts. But by doing what, I wonder.

'Ever been to Norway, Mr…?'

'Major Tor, My Prince, and no.'

He shrugs. 'No matter.' Then in a ridiculously off-hand sort of way, he tells me, 'There is a plot to murder the king of Sweden and your job is to put a stop to it.'

I feel my jaw bolt loosen, my chin clanking to my chest.

'Let me tell you a story.' The prince sits on his father's throne, shifting the sleeping wolf to his lap. It looks very comfortable there. 'Many years ago, the country of Denmark, my country, owned the country of Norway. But in 1814, with Sweden planning to invade us, we signed Norway over to the

Swedish, to pacify them, you see.'

I nod. Then, loftily, 'I did know of this, Sire.'

'Good. Good.' But his eyelids twitch like a bull bothered by a fly. 'Norway had no say in this whatsoever but it secretly hoped it was the first step to independence. Unfortunately for them, Sweden thought differently. The Swedish allow Norway to have a government, but it is a puppet government at best, and every attempt by Norway to separate the two lands has been brutally crushed.'

'But why assassinate Karl XV?'

'The plotters hope if the Swedish king is murdered and Norway is blamed, Sweden will threaten to attack it. Norway can then turn to Denmark, to my father, the king, to help protect it from the nasty Swedish.'

'Then there will be war.' I say flatly. 'Much blood will be spilt.'

'Yes, Major, it will. But, sadly, the plotters see it differently. They think Sweden will be too scared to attack Denmark as well.' He barks a laugh. 'Then my father's supposed to hand Norway over to Norway.'

'The first step to independence.' I mutter.

'Exactly. Blind fools! They will plunge the three lands into a foolhardy war and Sweden will win. It is too powerful, and when I'm king I will end up not the ruler of Denmark, but of a tiny prison cell, my only subjects, lice and the odd furry rat...'

'Spiders too,' I interject helpfully. I wither under his frosty look. 'But, er, your father, the king, can he not just refuse to help Norway; allow Sweden to attack them?'

'Sadly, my father is very old school.' He tuts disdainfully. 'It is not in his character to turn his back on the needy.'

I nod, not in agreement but to show my understanding. It seems the Crown Prince of Denmark is no fan of his king.

Bluntly, I ask him, 'Do you know who the assassin is?'

'Yes, I do.' There is a pause, for effect, perhaps. 'Locust.'

I frown. 'I beg your pardon?'

'Ah, yes, I forgot to tell you, there is an organization called SWARM; assassins for hire. Locust is a member and my spy tells me he is the man who has been given the job of murdering the Swedish king. Be warned, Major, he will be a very skilled killer and not easily stopped. He will not just fall in your lap like a ripe plumapple.'

I blanch. How did he forget to tell me this? 'And who's the crazy fool paying SWARM?' I muster.

'I very much doubt he's crazy,' growls the prince. Then his shoulders droop and he rocks his heels on the wooden floor. 'I

71

do not know, perhaps a man with a hankering for older better days. But he must be filthy rich if he can afford to pay SWARM.' Idly, he rubs his wolf's strawy fur and will not meet my eyes.

How odd and I ponder how it is he knows the cost of a SWARM assassin.

I watch him for a moment. There is, I think, a sort of shifty manner to this Danish prince: the way he chews so vehemently on his top lip and plays endlessly with the silver buttons on his tunic. Colonel Fiquet had been correct: he is a sly fox; a man who enjoys power, a man full of secrets and a man not to put too much trust in.

'Every year, a noble family is sent from Norway to Sweden to pay respects to the Swedish king on his birthday,' he tells me. 'This year, it is the turn of Duke Solbakken of Oslo. By the way, he's only a duke in Sweden's eyes; Norway abolished the aristocracy in 1821.'

I nod my understanding. Good for Norway, I think. I hate the aristocracy. To me, the blood of a king or a lord is no different to any man's blood and being royal is no guarantee of being trustworthy or honourable.

'He will be travelling to your capital city, Stockholm, with his wife, his daughter and his son. My spy tells me it is a member of the family who is this Locust. I know the duke well, a forgetful fellow, often lost in his own library, so I agreed to send him a Swedish trooper to show him the way and to keep him and his family safe on the long trip. That is your cover story, Major.

'Your actual task is to discover who in the family is the assassin and stop him.' His eyes narrow to evil slits. 'Kill him, if you must.'

'Or her,' I add.

The prince nods slowly. 'Or her. Nobody in the Solbakken family knows the truth of why I'm sending you. I suggest you look to the son. Never met him but he's a bit of a rebel or so I'm told; probably be him. If you succeed, there will be a reward of a hundred Danish kronor.'

I blink and try to swallow my greedy hunger. This is a kingly sum; almost two years pay for a mercenary. But even if I do stop Locust, I ponder, will SWARM not just send a second assassin to do the job. I almost put this to Frederick but I stop myself. Not my problem. 'The spy you speak of; perhaps he can help me.'

'No, SWARM murdered him. They sent me his eyeballs in a box of English toffees.'

I blink, my lips forming a perfect 'O'. 'How, er, awful,' I

stumble.

'Indeed.' The prince nods, a cruel smile curling his lips. 'I much prefer mints.'

Frederick, it seems, is not a man to be shackled by the chains of empathy.

Gulping, I begin to massage my temple with my fingertips.

'Major, I admit this job is risky, so, if you stop Locust for me, on top of the hundred kronor, I will reward you with this.'

He draws his sword and shows it to me: it is shiny and slim, almost willowy in fact, with a ruby-encrusted gold hilt. I can almost feel the power oozing off it, bewitching me.

'History calls this sword Tyrfing. Forged by the dwarf, Dvalinn, it will never rust and can cut through rock. But legend has it Dvalinn cursed it to do three evil deeds.' He eyes me devilishly. 'Or so they say.'

The steel seems to glimmer and spark and I half expect it to catch fire.

'Agreed,' I snap, fighting the urge to snatch it off him. This prince can sell dirt to a ditch digger.

'Good! Off you trot, then. The Flying Spur will carry you to Norway and Duke Solbakken is expecting you. Don't mess this up, Major. I expect to attend a birthday party on the 19th, not a royal funeral.'

The wolf growls, a sleepy eye snapping open, underlining the menace in his words. The prince pats his bristled-up fur.

For just a moment, I waver on the spot, wondering if perhaps Frederick will agree to a written contract. But, no; he will not want there to be any proof of a Danish royal employing a mercenary to kill assassins. The word of a prince must do.

I bow and march over to the door. But there, I stop. 'Sire, if I may be so bold, how is it you know of SWARM?'

Frederick looks up and, to my surprise, I see a shadow of terror there. 'It's complicated, but let's just say they did a small job for me a few years ago. Oh, and Major, remember this, they never miss. Ever.'

Wednesday, 9th September, 1870
10 Days to Assassination Day

0820 hours, Oslo, Norway

Two days later, I canter up a stony path and by a mossy statue

of the Swedish king to the Solbakken family villa. It is very majestic-looking with big, stern-looking windows in yellow wooden walls and a brass-knobbed, brass-knockered door. There is a cart parked in front of the villa, just by the steps. It has red wheels and is piled up with trunks.

The Flying Spur had dutifully dropped me in Norway but far to the south west and a long way from the capital city of Oslo. It seems the small purse of silver Frederick's trooper had left on Skipper Church's flabby lap only covered dropping me 'on his way' and not 'out of his way'.

Miserly git!

For a day and a night I had travelled north, passing through a host of tiny hamlets: Larvik, Tönsberg, Hortén and Drammen, till finally, with blistered buttocks, I had arrived in Oslo.

Stopping to post Colonel Fiquet's letter to his mother, I had been told how to find the Solbakken residence. 'Go west,' the rheumy-eyed postmaster had told me, his moustache so curly it had tickled the corners of his mouth. 'Just up the hill there. The size of a baron's castle. You can't miss it.'

And I had to agree with him; I had seen the rooftop from a mile away.

Trotting up to the villa, I spy a tiny low-walled cemetery

lorded over by a splendid ivory-white crypt. There is a tiny wooden cross too, half hidden in a nettle patch in the corner. A pet, perhaps, or a hapless uncle who enjoyed his whisky too much and embarrassed the Solbakkens with foul limericks at family funerals.

Spotting a bucket of water, I clamber off my poor, pooped horse and pull him over to it. There, I let him drink. Then I step over to a patch of clover, pull off a leaf, spit on it and begin to polish my boots.

Well, I don't want to look too scruffy when I meet the duke.

'OY! YOU!' A burly man in a butler's uniform lumbers doggishly over to me. Oddly, the cuffs of his shirt only just cover his elbows and his trousers ride up to his shins. 'Whatever y' peddling, his Lordship's not interest. Now, be off with y'.'

'I'm not peddling anything,' I say sternly. 'I'm here to see Duke Solbakken.'

The butler's owlish eyes, tinted yellow, gaze doubtfully on my muddy tunic and scuffed boots. I feel like a horse being looked over in a paddock and I wonder if he will ask to see my teeth.

Blixt stomps his hoof; this man is making him jumpy.

'It's important.' I back up my words by resting my hand on my sword. Oddly, I feel a little jumpy too. He reminds me uncomfortably of a troll out of a terrifying childhood tale - and he smells of muddy dog.

'I er, see, Sir.' He is English, a Londoner perhaps, and sort of spits the 'Sir'. 'Do follow me.'

Dutifully, I chase him up the steps to the villa. There, by the brass-knockered, brass-knobbed door, I see a dumpy-looking man with sallow cheeks, muddy-brown eyes and mad-professor hair. He has on a scarlet silk tunic decorated with fluffy cuffs and a gold watch, and all of his fingers, all of them, sport a ring with a plum-sized gem.

'A, er, gentleman to see you, My Lord.' He spits the 'gentleman' too.

'Don't call me 'My Lord' you fool. This is Norway, not Sweden.' He rubs his temple. 'I just can't find the staff.'

The butler bows his apology but I spy a tiny ember of fury in his eyes.

My brow furrows. Then I remember the Danish prince telling me Norway had abolished aristocracy. A slip perhaps; I recall Prince Frederick's words: '...a hankering for older, better days'.

The duke eyeballs me crossly, puffing out his chest and

tucking his thumbs in his pockets. 'I'm just off to Sweden,' he tells me, self-importantly. 'Stockholm, in fact, for the king's birthday party. So I'm not in the market for any silks or...'

'My name is Major Tor,' I interrupt him, beginning to get mildly annoyed. I'm in a cavalryman's uniform, not a shopkeeper's apron. 'The Crown Prince of Denmark sent me to...'

'Yes, yes,' his eyes widen and he snaps his ring-laden fingers, 'I remember now. Our shepherd to Stockholm. Very decent of young Frederick, I must say. We play chess, you know.'

'Poker too. He told me.'

'Yes, yes, poker too - and chess.' The duke seems a little upset by my butting in and inexplicably shoots the butler a nervy look.

A young woman walks over, her long legs hidden in jodhpurs and knee-length boots. She is tall and willowy and has a rabbity spring to her step. 'Is this the daring knight sent to protect us?' she asks the duke. There is a rhythmic lilt to her speech; the Oslo accent, I suspect.

'Yes, my sweet, this is, er...'

'Tor,' the butler gently reminds him, noticeably skipping

my rank.

I shoot him a daggery look.

'Yes, yes, Tor, and this is my daughter, Astrid.'

I bow and her lips curl up. It is the sort of smile you want to keep. She smells good too; warm and spicy like Christmas, and she has a sort of monkey twinkle to her eye as if any second now she will pinch her dad's bottom, blow a raspberry and run off and climb a tree.

'Sir,' it is the butler by my elbow, 'everything is packed…'

'But my socks,' yelps the duke. 'I must not forget my socks. It can be terribly cold in Sweden in September.' He talks so fast, it reminds me of rain pattering on a tin roof.

'In the wagon, Sir, with the present for the Swedish king.'

'What, all of them?'

'Yes, Sir.'

'All sixty-six? Even the pair with the tiny snowmen on?'

'Yes, Sir.'

'And my silk tunic with the sparkly buttons?'

'You're wearing it, Sir.'

'Oh, yes,' the absentminded duke pats his chest, 'so I am. Excellent! Excellent!' He looks to me and frowns. 'So, er…'

'Tor.' Astrid blows a curl out of her eyes. Glossy as silk spun by caterpillars.

'Yes, yes, silly me. Memory of a, er...'

His daughter's hands discover her hips. 'Goldfish, Father.'

'Yes, yes, a goldfish. Well, er, Tor, enjoy the trip; probably not much for you to do...'

'Unless we bump into highwaymen,' I cut him off.

He cocks an eyebrow, wondering perhaps if I'm joking with him. Looking awfully nervy, he hops from foot to foot, two of his rings slipping off and clinking to the steps. I wonder if he is excited or merely has chronic diarrhoea.

'Excellent! Excellent! Let's be off, then.' Snatching up the errant rings, he hastens over to the wagon and hops up on it, squeezing up to a tall lady in a fluffy mink scarf. She must be his wife, the Duchess Solbakken.

'My father is very excited to meet the Swedish king,' Astrid tells me.

'God knows why,' mutters a weedy-looking youth, mooching past us. He is a small man, a tiny man, a dwarf, but I glimpse a long curved dagger hooked in his belt.

'Bertil, my very annoying younger brother,' Astrid enlightens me.

'I see.' My suspect! I remember my father told me never to trust crooks, kings and tiny men.

'He's a pig,' the daughter tells me matter-of-factly, 'but

81

only on a good day.'

I suppress a grin. 'Is today a good day?'

'For me, yes. For him,' her eyes flash, 'it is not.'

I watch the son drag his feet over to the wagon and climb up. The duchess attempts to playfully pinch his cheek but he pulls away, his milky almond eyes glowing with contempt. He has the alert, dangerous look of a cat that can smell a nest of baby mice.

What a charming lad. Ironically, he reminds me of the lord's son I killed only three years ago. My poor, sweet sister...

'I can tell by your accent you're Swedish, but your tunic's French cavalry. Tell me, Major,' the daughter eyes me curiously, 'who is your master?'

She spotted I'm a major too. I'm impressed. She knows her uniforms.

'The chap with the deepest pockets,' I reply equally sternly.

She nods and the corners of her lips tip up. 'I thought so.' But there is little malice in her tone.

Interestingly, Astrid is not travelling on the wagon with her family. She jumps nimbly up on a chestnut horse and kicks the heels of her felt-topped riding boots, trotting off.

I gaze after her, a buffalo tap-dancing in my chest. Wow!

Standing by the waving butler, we watch the laden wagon swagger away. Surprisingly, Duke Solbakken is driving and I wonder why there's no chauffeur. Sweeping by us, my eyes meet Bertil's and I see venom there.

'Swedish buffoon,' he mutters, just for me.

'How sweet,' I murmur.

All of a sudden, the duke pulls the wagon up and jumps off. 'My golf clubs,' he yelps, scampering back up the path.

Astrid stops too; she looks annoyed, her fist clenched on her riding crop. Perhaps she enjoys a spot of golf too and is upset her scatty dad almost left the clubs in Oslo.

The frazzled duke scoots past us. I suck on my bottom lip; he's off to Sweden in September, not Italy in June. 'This is going to be a very long trip,' I say.

The butler by my elbow nods. 'Yes, Sir, it is. For you, anyway,' he adds cryptically.

I eye him for a moment, noting his big shoulders, bulldog jaw and long spindly fingers; they look all wrinkly as if he pickled them in brine.

I will try to talk to him; a little man-to-man banter. 'The er, tiny wooden cross over there in the cemetery; was it a pet?'

The butler scowls and nods.

'A rabbit or a…?'

'Hamster.'

'Oh.' What a jolly fellow he is; he reeks too. And I'm upwind! Subtly, I shuffle a little to my left.

Duke Solbakken shoulders by me with his clubs and we watch him scurry over to the duchess and hand them up to her. Two balls drop from the pockets and I catch the butler flinch.

'My sister had a hamster,' I tell him. 'Was yours a er, boy or a…'

'Boy!' he spits. He turns on me crossly. 'Brown fur, six whiskers, played on his wheel and munched a lot of walnuts. In turn, he was munched on by Bertil's cat. Astrid was very upset. Happy?'

'Very.'

'I can fetch her new hamster, if you wish me to. She calls him Elephant. Why? Who knows. Do I want to know? Not particularly.'

I show him my palms. 'No! Honestly.'

'Then I will return to my work.' He storms up the steps. Well, it's always nice to meet new people.

With iron-filled boots, I walk over to fetch my horse. The blisters on my buttocks will not be happy, a perfect match for my mood.

Saturday, 12th September, 1870
7 Days to Assassination Day

1435 hours, just west of Karlstad, Sweden

Slumped in my saddle, my horse trots after the bouncing bottom of the Solbakken's wagon. The duke seems very keen to get to the king's birthday party on the 19th so we only stop for food and to sleep: hot eels in a drafty, spider-ridden castle in Björkelangen, pickled whelks in a smelly pub in Åmatfors (there I had awoken to find a rat sleeping in my boot) and sheep's trotters in a torp, a sort of tiny hut, in Arvika, where the thin walls did little to stop the howl and 'Yip, yip, yip' of a hungry fox.

On the afternoon of the fourth day, we meander our way past Vänern, the biggest lake in Sweden. I look wistfully to the glassy water shimmering in the autumn sun; it looks deceptively warm and after so long on the road, I fancy a dip to wash off the dirt. But there's no way the fretful duke will

let us stop.

Slowly, the day slips by, everything I see and smell reminding me of how wonderful Sweden is and how much I miss it. I spot badgers hunting frogs and worms by the water and a deer chewing on the bark of a dwarf birch tree. We even cross the path of a moose, his petal-shaped ears popping up from a well-chewed rose hip bush.

I know my mind should be focused on the job of determining who in the Solbakken family the assassin is, but it's not. For here I am, the scent of pine trees in my nostrils, returning to my beloved Sweden after so many years. I had been in the Swedish army back then, only a lowly corporal, but murdering a lord's son had destroyed my career. I had been forced to flee. Better a life on the run than a short trip and a sudden stop on the end of a hangman's rope.

We clomp by a daisy patch, the ivory petals exploding from penny-sized balls. To me they look like tiny suns hidden in the grass. I remember in the summers how my sister had enjoyed making daisy bracelets; much too twiddly a job for my banana thumbs...

My thoughts start to drift but I stop myself, cursing the way my mind can still savage me with the memory of Sylva.

I just hope nobody will recognize me in Stockholm. No, I

need not worry. My sorry tale had happened in Jokkmokk, far to the north of Sweden.

I do up the top button of my tunic. The sun is doing her very best to keep me warm but the wind is icy cold and seems determined to win the war. It sandpapers my cheeks, freezing the tip of my chin. I remember, I always enjoyed Swedish Septembers, chilly, but the paths hidden under wonderfully leafy red and yellow hills and the snow still a month or two away.

I eye the Solbakken family huddled up in the wagon. The duchess is driving now. Fifty or so, she is a tall lady, dwarfing the poor duke, his chin barely level with her swelling bosom. She has big hands too, almost manly, and a knobbly wart sits shivering on the lid of her left eye. There is a tulip in her hair but it looks oddly out of place. I mull over the thought that perhaps she is trying to soften her bullish looks. If so, the effect is similar to putting a flowery dress on Djingis Khan. Unusually, for a duchess, she has rotten teeth too.

She is hunched over and when we had stopped for lunch I had spotted her eyes were smudged black like a panda's. But the son, I see, is too lazy to help her and the duke is dozing. I frown; a little peculiar that. No driver, the butler had stayed in Oslo and I had seen no sign of any servants at the villa. Is the

duke broke, I wonder, and cannot afford any staff.

Only the son is facing my way. Every now and then he shoots me a viperish glare, but I'm unperturbed by the strength of his hatred, so I just chuckle and grin. I know it will annoy him the most.

Reluctantly, my sleepy mind returns to the job at hand and begins to pick and pry at the problem: so, who is the assassin? Not the duke, he's just a dithery old man with a goldfish's memory. And not the daughter, she's just too pretty to be a murderess. I wonder how old she is: twenty-three, twenty-four...

Just then, embarrassingly, Astrid trots up. I feel my cheeks glow red under my dusty skin; a schoolboy with a silly crush.

'How did you cut your cheek?' she asks me. Rather boldly, I think.

'Shaving,' I respond carelessly. I'm trying to be aloof but who am I kidding. I can storm a castle, no problem, but chat up a girl...

'You know, if you try using a razor and not a blunt scythe.' I suspect she is trying to smoother a giggle.

We trot on in silence. 'So, is it just Tor, or Tor blah, blah, blah...?'

'Just Tor,' I watch the breeze toss a maple leaf over a bush, 'or Major.'

'I see.'

I doubt she can. A surname only spells 'f-o-o-l-h-a-r-d-y' to a criminal on the run.

'Well, Just Tor, it was very sweet of the Danish prince to send you all the way from Copenhagen to protect us.'

'Yes, it was.'

'The musket in your saddle holster there looks as if it'd stop a bull elephant.'

'Big is not always better,' I say pompously. 'A sunflower is no better than a violet.' Then, in a burst of idiocy, I add, 'I never shot a bull elephant.' Thus implying I had shot a different sort of elephant, which, of course, I had not.

'He's paying you well, I hope. The Prince.'

'Very.'

'You don't say a lot, do you?'

My collar suddenly feels awfully tight. 'No,' I muster pathetically. I wonder if there's a book, The A to Z of Lemons, and if I'm in there under T.

Shooting me a tiny smile, she rolls her eyes, shimmering lagoons and easy for a man to drown in. I spot a hint of yellow in them and I wonder, idly, if she is ill.

For a thoughtful second I thumb the steel hilt of my sword.

I'm trying to remember who also has yellow-tinted eyes. I frown; a person I had met only recently…

'ABSURD!' bellows Bertil and the spell is broken.

I lift my own eyes to the wagon. Solbakken's stroppy son is standing up, his fists clenched, a leer twisting his lips. 'He's not even our king,' he is yelling. 'He's the king of the enemy.'

'Stop it!' barks the duke, standing up too and swiping at his son's lazy curls. 'Karl XV is a powerful man. A fool, yes, but powerful. Never forget, he is the ruler of our lands too.'

'Denmark is the true ally of Norway,' Bertil snarls back, 'not Sweden. King Karl will never allow us to be independent. But the Crown Prince of Denmark, when he is king…'

My ears prick up.

'Bertil, do shut up.' It is the duchess's turn to reprimand him, her words a scalpel. 'Soon we will be in Stockholm, in the King's Castle. Karl is our monarch now; it is disloyal to say such things.'

'Disloyal!' Bertil's eyes widen in incredulity; he is almost trembling with zealotry. 'DISLOYAL!'

'And keep in mind, son,' the duke butts in, his bony bottom rediscovering the softly padded bench, 'this is Sweden now. If a spy of King Karl heeds your words, you will very soon be enjoying the comforts of a Swedish jail.'

This seems to do the trick and, fuming, Bertil sits too.

Interesting. The son seems to despise the Swedish. It is so obviously Bertil who is the assassin. The Prince of Denmark is correct in suspecting him, but I wonder how Frederick knows. I remember he told me, he had never even met the boy.

But it all seems so perfect, so easy and I cannot help feeling the Solbakken family had just put on a theatrical show, and the show had been for me.

I resist the urge to clap.

'Ignore him.' Astrid taps my leg with her riding crop. 'He's just upset. He wanted to stay in Oslo and go drinking with his pals.'

I nod. She mistakenly thinks I'm upset by his treacherous words. I'm Swedish, after all.

But how can Bertil be Locust, a member of this 'oh, so elite' SWARM? He's only eighteen or so and he still has spots. I recall the Danish prince telling me the assassins never miss. The only thing this lad would never miss is a trip to the pub.

But my conjecturing is sadly interrupted by a highwayman

and his crossbow. Always the way, I find.

'Drop your pistol, Trooper. Good boy. Now, slowly, sloooowly climb off the horse.'

Obediently, I drop to the leafy path and look to the robber. I'm met with ferrety eyes, rotten teeth and wind-raw cheeks. I spot the index finger on his left hand is missing, sawn off at the knuckle like a missing key on a piano. He has on a dirty, patched-up tunic and scuffed clogs on his feet. I gather he is not the most successful of crooks.

I spot a second highwayman over by the wagon. He is holding a cocked pistol up to the duke's chest. And then a third robber, up on the hill to my left.

'Now unbuckle the sword or I put this arrow in your eye.'

He is Swedish, so I will try and talk to him. 'God dag, min herre,' I begin in a chatty sort of way. 'Now, there's no need to hurt anybody…'

'I'm not your pal,' he spits, 'and I think there is.' Cuffing me with the butt of the crossbow, I drop to my knees, seeing stars.

'You too, Lass,' he's giving orders to Astrid now, 'off you jump.'

'I'm a lady, Sir, and a lady needs a helping hand.'

Snorting, the robber steps over me. 'Always happy to help

92

a lady,' he says slimily.

Clawing at my throbbing brow, I look up to see Astrid's boot hammer the robber's chin. With a startled cry, he cartwheels back, tripping over me and thudding to the path.

My God! The crossbow.

On all fours, I scurry over to the stunned crook, but Astrid is quicker. She scampers by me and with a wolfish howl she kicks the crossbow from his hand. Then she drops to a knee and rams a dagger up to his left eye. Despite the pain I'm in, I still wonder where she had hidden it. 'Try anything,' she growls, 'anything, and you will discover how little of a lady I truly am.'

With the unhappy knowledge that the battle is yet to be won, I clamber shakily to my feet. But I do not need to worry. The dithery old duke is not looking dithery at all and has a sword up to the second robber's chest. I look up the hill and spy the last of the crooks scampering up it.

Slightly cross-eyed, I watch Bertil jump to his feet, a dagger clutched in his paw. 'NO!' I cry, but a split second later, the shaft of the blade is wedged deeply in the fleeing man's back.

'Rotten coward,' I muster. For there is no victory to be had in murdering a man who is running away.

With blood dripping on my cheek, I drop to my knees and slowly, painfully slowly, roll over onto my back. And there I lay, just next to the red wheel of the Solbakken's cart, two thoughts battling for supremacy in my mind. Firstly, it seems every member of the family, barring perhaps the old duchess, has the skills to be Locust, and, secondly, why can I see a tiny wooden coffin?

2123 hours, the Wily Wolf Inn, Karlstad

'STOP!'

I'm back in the galley on the Flying Spur. The Japanese cook, his thin lips cruelly twisted, pays no heed to my cry for mercy and lobs a pan of snapping lobster at me.

Instinctively, I duck.

'Soon you will feel the sting of Wasp,' he tells me softly, his words brimming with malice.

I see a girl; a girl I know. She is blindfolded and lashed to the stove. In horror, I watch the cook snatch up a pot of bubbling water and step over to her.

94

I drop to my knees. 'Don't do this,' I beseech him. 'There's no honour in it.' But there is only murder in his eyes.

There must be a way to stop him. I must stop him. I want to stop him but I'm frozen…

With a cackling cry, he tips up the pot.

'SYLVA!' I cry.

My eyes snap open.

'Shush now, Trooper. Shush.'

Thankfully, I'm not on the Flying Spur but in a bedroom in a four-poster bed, and by my elbow, perched on a stool, is Duke Solbakken's daughter. Gingerly, I try to sit up, Astrid hopping to her feet to help me and to puff up my pillows.

I rally up a tiny rasping, 'Thanks.' The pillow is soft, the blanket warm but scratchy on my chin.

I spot a mirror on the far wall and even from here I can see the chicken's egg bump on my brow. Gently, I prod it and wince. What with the bump, my cut cheek, hollow eyes and chipped front teeth, I look a mess - trampled on by a bull and run over by a cart. I just hope Colonel Fiquet was correct and women really did worship men with scars.

My eyes drift to a yellow flower on the window sill, then over to my tunic laying on a sofa in the corner, and by the legs, my boots.

95

'Did you undress me?' I mutter, eyeing her suspiciously.

'No, I did not,' she shoots back indignantly. 'I'm the daughter of a duke, not a doorman, and my Uncle Ivor invented the toothpick.' Her lips twitch but there is no trace of a blush. 'It so happens the town doctor did. He dressed your cheek too. It looked a little er, gooey.'

'Gooey!' I blow out my cheeks. 'That's just wonderful.'

'Anyway, he told me, sternly, to tell you, sternly, to stay in bed and rest.'

'I only wish.' I sit up stiffly. 'Can you hand me my tunic and boots? Oh, and shut your eyes; no peeking,' I add in my best schoolmaster's tenor.

Feeling dizzy, I slowly put them on. Then, I shuffle over to the sofa and sit.

'So, tell me, what happened to the highwaymen?'

'Can I open my eyes now?' She is playing with me.

'Yes.'

Dropping her hand to her lap, she skips over and sits by me on the sofa, curling up her long, 'LOOOONG' legs.

'We strapped two of them to the wagon,' she tells me matter-of-factly, 'and we took them here.'

I scowl. 'Here being…?'

'Oh, yes, sorry, here being the Wily Wolf Inn in Karlstad.'

She drops her eyes. 'You er, threw up all the way to town.'

'Oh. Sorry.' So much for romance. 'It's the blood, you see. It upsets my stomach.'

'It was your blood.'

'Yes. Yes, I know. Particularly upsetting.'

She looks at me incredulously. 'But I thought you were a mercenary. You must see blood every day.'

'I'm not a butcher,' I tell her defensively. Then I nod. 'It is, I admit, a bit of a handicap.'

'A bit!'

Thoroughly embarrassed, I show her my palms. 'So, where did you put the crooks?'

'The Swedish police took them off to the town lockup.' She says this very quickly and will not meet my eye.

'Hmm,' I scratch my stubbly chin, wondering why she is lying, 'and what happened to the poor chap Bertil murdered?'

'He hardly murdered him,' shoots off Astrid, coming to the defense of her brother. 'The scoundrel was trying to rob us.'

'He was trying to run away,' I snap back mercilessly. 'Hardly the act of d'Artagnan.'

'Sorry?'

'You know, the hero in The Three Musketeers.' I sigh. 'Well, I suppose it is a bit of a boys' book.'

97

She balloons her cheeks and rubs her eye tiredly. 'Anyway, we left him on the hill.'

'Food for the crows,' I mutter, remembering Jacob.

She nods. 'Food for the crows.'

We sit silently for a moment, then, desperate for her not to go, I blurt out, 'The plant on the window sill over there is a mattlummer. Lycopodium clavatum,' I add lamely, 'in er, Latin.' I mentally kick myself. Why did I not just compliment her eyes or tell her how wonderful she smells. I'm such a nerd.

Her lips quirk up. 'The flowers remind me of tiny cobs of corn.'

'Yes, they do. They do!' I nod enthusiastically. 'And if you throw them in the fire they will sizzle and explode.'

'Excellent for fireworks then.'

'Yes, excellent.' Wow! She actually finds my interest in flowers interesting. But play it cool. Play it cool.

'I never thought I'd meet a flower-loving mercenary,' she tells me.

I smile. 'I grew up in Jokkmokk in the very north of Sweden. Winters tend to drag on there so when I was a boy I always watched for the first tulips and buttercups. When they blossomed I knew summer was on the way. I guess a flower to me is warmth and light; long days, short nights.'

'Less time to dream,' she mutters. She pulls absentmindedly on the sleeve of her cardigan, covering her balled-up fist.

I look to her curiously. What a very odd thing to say. But a second later her wall is back up, her armour back on.

I watch her play fretfully with a button and I decide to let it go.

'You did well, by the way,' I say to her, 'kicking that robber on the chin.' Then, mimicking her words, 'I never thought I'd meet a duchess's daughter who's handy in a scrap.'

She grins, her mood lifting. 'I went to a school run by nuns. We did mostly bible study, knitting and Kong fu.'

I tut and she winks playfully at me. 'So tell me, where did you hide the knife? In your saddle?'

'Oh no.' She looks to me all innocent-eyed. 'In my bloomers. Sister Mary told me it's the last place a robber will think to look.'

I chuckle. 'Only if the robber happens to be a nun,' I mutter to my boots.

I go to stand up but her next words stop me. 'When you slept, you yelled, Sylva.'

'She's my sister.' I clench my jaw and correct my grammar. 'She was my sister.'

'Was?'

I feel my guard drop under her sympathetic gaze and soft soprano; honey from a pot.

'A yob, drunk on vodka, was galloping full pelt and knocked her over, killing her; the murderer never even stopped to help. She was just seven. Pretty as a daffodil but a real tomboy too. I remember she always had rocks in her pockets and twigs in her curls.' A whimper slips from my lips. 'Seven forever, now. Forever young.'

Her lips quiver in a fleeting, sad smile. 'I'm so sorry.'

I nod silently, thanking her for her sympathy. It feels warm and comforting like chicken soup. 'He was the son of Lord Gripenstedt,' I tell her, 'and this lord had very deep pockets, so he bribed the judge and the son got off scot free. I challenged the murderer to a duel but the coward refused,' I rub my brow, the memory tormenting me, 'so I marched up to him, pulled my musket and shot him in the eye. Then I went on the run from the hangman's noose.'

Saying it now, it all seems so 'run of the mill': a trip to Jokkmokk wool market, a picnic by the river, shooting Lord Gripenstedt's cowardly son in cold blood. But that day my life had broken up like ice on a river at the touch of spring.

'Hardly the act of er,' Astrid frowns, 'D'Artagnan did you say?'

Her hand finds my knee, perhaps trying to lessen the punch to her jaw-thumping words. But there's no need. I know there is much truth to what she says. When I shot Gripenstedt's son, he had not even drawn his pistol. How is that any better than Bertil murdering a man who was trying to run away?

'Touché,' I mutter. The truth still hurts.

Mindful of the softness of her touch, I suddenly feel awfully hot and clammy and I tug violently on my tunic collar.

'You must miss your parents terribly,' she says softly.

I nod. She pulls her hand away but my skin still feels all tingly just there. With difficulty, I swallow. 'Mostly Mum. In May when I was a boy, we planted tulip bulbs in the flower beds and in summer we went berry picking...' I chatter on: snowdrops by the pond, a rather belligerent holly bush seemingly determined to smoother Dad's tool shed. But I do not tell her how I worry if I ever fold up my uniform and return to Jokkmokk, my days will turn insufferably dull, old dry muffins, not sharp and sweet like my mum's rhubarb crumble.

'Dad, he worked on a ship, he always had a book for me from his travels. Usually a history book: The History of Art, The History of Ships, The History of, well, whatever took his fancy. By ten I knew a Turner from a Monet and a schooner from a cutter. Artist and ships,' I answer her scowl.

'But the father, this Lord Gripenstedt,' Astrid gently interrupts my reminiscing, 'if he ever sees you…'

'It happened in Jokkmokk, a three week trek from here.' I smile confidently. 'Nobody knows me in Stockholm.'

'Well, just don't go to the king's birthday party.'

I look to her, stumped. 'Why not?'

'Why not! Trooper, think. You killed the son of a Swedish lord, yes?'

'Yes.'

'Tor, every lord in Sweden is going to be at that party.'

~

The bar in the Wily Wolf reeks of beer and old men. It is stuffy and hot too, packed to the rafters with pipe-puffing woodsmen and travellers in need of a bed. I spot Duke Solbakken and his wife in a dimly lit corner, well armed with tankards and a flagon of ale. Bertil, I see, is in the pub too, but he is propping up the bar, chatting up a pretty girl in a patched-up yellow dress.

The duke spots me and beckons me over with a wave. Reluctantly, I walk over to them, my boots almost cementing to the beer-splattered floor. I still feel dizzy but I try not to knock over too many stools on the way. I don't want them to think I'm a bungling fool - and a drunk.

'How do you feel?' he asks me in his usual nervy chatter. 'Better I hope. Excellent! Excellent! My, that's a nasty lump on your brow there.'

'I'm a lot better, thanks to you, Sir.' My eyes narrow as I say, 'You were pretty handy with that sword.'

He shows me a set of shimmering teeth. 'It was all very exciting, I must say, er....'

'Tor,' I help him.

'Yes! Yes! Corporal Tor.' With a wave of his hand, three of his rings fly off and he knocks over his tankard of beer. 'Oh my, how clumsy of me.'

Watching Duke Solbakken try to mop up the frothy mess, I recall how the highwayman had had the pistol shoved up to his chest. The duke must have drawn his sword awfully fast to stop the robber from firing.

I begin to wonder if this clumsiness of his - and his poor

memory - is not just an elaborate act to put me off the scent.

'Tell me, Tor,' his wife's posh Oslo accent interrupts my distrustful thoughts, 'can we expect to bump into any other highwayman on our trip?'

I look to the duchess, her flint eyes frozen and cold, and arch a polite eyebrow. 'I wish I knew, My Lady.' This is Sweden so I can call her that now. 'There is still a long way to go,' I tell her.

'It was my understanding the Prince of Denmark sent you to protect us.'

I shuffle my feet. 'Yes, he did,' I say sheepishly.

She showers me with a full set of ebony teeth; a sword wrapped in velvet. 'Then it is your job - to know, is it not?'

Chastised, I drop my eyes to my boots and nod. 'Yes, My Lady.' I suspect this is the beginning of a bitter tongue lashing but, surprisingly, she dabs a lace hanky to her lips and turns away, seemingly content with my squirming reply.

'Well er, if you will excuse me, I must feed Blixt, my...'

'Feed yourself too,' the duke interrupts me from under the table. Presumably he's trying to find his rings. 'The moose hotpot here is excellent. Excellent!'

I nod. 'I will be in the barn if you need me.'

I mooch over to the door, Duchess Solbakken's eyes

crawling over my back. I feel a fool; a silly schoolboy in a classroom full of scholars.

'You see trooper-boy over there,' Bertil trumpets to the pub. 'His job is to protect me and my family, but he's a buffoon. All he can do is spew up.'

I know he's just trying to provoke me, but I still want to knock his teeth in.

Clenching my fists, I snatch a tin lantern off the window sill and shoulder open the door. Bertil's howls of mirth follow me from the inn but I know I must be the better man. Still, I do find myself contemplating how difficult it would be to jam this lantern up his noble bottom.

Not too difficult, I think. No, not too difficult at all.

It is dark out, the sky inky black with just a splash of cloud and dots of stars. With the dry autumn twigs splintering under my boots, I stroll by the low wall of a well, a bucket on a rope over the abyss, and over to a colossal red barn.

There, with the help of my lantern, I quickly find Blixt in a stall, but he seems perfectly happy, shoulder to shoulder with Astrid's chestnut mare, munching on an Everest of hay.

I think, perhaps, he's in love.

Popping the lantern up on a handy beer barrel, I fondly pat his furry rump. 'You must be shattered, old boy,' I tell him

sympathetically.

The lantern casts a spidery glow over a wooden wheelbarrow and just by it, the left red wheel of the Solbakken's cart. I scowl, the memory of what I had seen, lying in the dirt, puddle-jumping into my mind.

Uneasily, I walk over to the wagon and peer under it. There it is, the coffin-shaped box. It is still hooked firmly to the wood, but there's no rust so without any difficulty I unclip it, drawing it gently from under the wagon's dirt-splattered belly.

Carrying it over to the lantern on the barrel, I put it softly on the sawdust-covered floor. Then, dropping to a knee, I pry off the lid.

My scowl deepens; the box is crammed full of curved daggers. But, unnervingly, it is not the daggers that worry me the most. It is the rifle.

Gingerly, I pick it up and study it.

Considering the bulkiness of the scope and the span of the barrel, the musket feels almost feather-light. I scowl, recalling how the gunsmith in London had assured me the scope on my rifle was unique; his very own patent. But it now seems he had been a little sloppy with the truth. In fact, the scope on this weapon looks considerably more powerful.

My eyes narrow, calculating. I reckon the musket must be four, almost five feet from the tip of the butt to the top of the muzzle.

Recklessly, I pull back the lock, shoulder it and squeeze. Click! Empty. I look in the box; no powder and no shot.

Peering into the barrel, I marvel at the sheer size of it. You could shoot a rocket out of there, never mind a bullet. Anybody shot by this monster will undoubtedly feel the grim reaper's kiss…

A twig snaps!

Saved by three years of dodging bullets, I instinctively duck, a knife hammering into the beer barrel just by my cheek. Dropping the rifle, I filch a dagger from the box and crawl over to the wheelbarrow.

I cower there.

The seconds tick by and, warily, I peer over the top.

I immediately spy the silhouette of a man over by the door of the barn. He is perfectly still; I suspect he is hunting the shadows for a target. The moon glints off a silvery object in his hand and my spirits plummet. A second knife!

With the help of my disloyal lantern, his sharp eyes find me.

He's preparing to throw it, but today, driven by terror, I'm faster.

But throwing daggers is about on par with my swordsmanship and it tomahawks harmlessly off his chest.

'You know, Major, you must be the poorest trooper I ever met.' It is Bertil; I recognise the weepy drawl.

He swaggers over to me, a kick of his boot sending the wheelbarrow flying. I try to scamper away, but all too soon he is standing over me, my back to the barrel, his lips snarled up in a victory snarl.

'This is the tanto dagger,' he says conversationally. 'Very popular with the Japanese ninja.'

Why is he telling me this, I wonder. But I know why. He's enjoying himself; a cat playing with a mouse.

'To think he sent you to kill me,' he sneers, his eyes wild, craving for blood. 'What a joke.'

He knows, I think. MY GOD! HE KNOWS!

Suddenly, I remember the dagger he had first thrown at me. My eyes shoot left. There it is, the blade still lodged in the wood. I yank it out and let fly.

There then follows the longest second in history.

Mesmerized, I watch his clawing hands and the tiny drop of blood dribbling from his lips to his chin. Then, the spark in his eyes sputters and flickers out and with hardly a whimper,

he folds to the floor.

Watchfully, I creep over to him. I drop to a knee and press two fingers to his wrist. I can find no pulse but what I do find is the familiar tattoo of a spider. My eyes spin, my mind suddenly swamped with the vipery eyes of the Japanese cook on the Flying Spur. So he had been a member of SWARM too!

But now I know what to look for.

I also remember the low wall of the well. Ruthlessly, I drag Bertil's limp body over to it and drop him in there. There is no splash, just a dull thud. There must be no water in it which is probably for the best; he'd only float like a turd. Then I kick away the scuff marks left in the dirt by the heels of his dragging boots.

Jogging back over to the barn, I urgently grab up the rifle and replace it in the box. I then hook it back under the belly of the wagon. I stop for a moment, allowing my mind to play catch up, but I can only think of two ways of doing this: tell the duke I killed his son, or…

I hurry over to the stall and much to the annoyance of Blixt, I let his buddy go free. For a second or two, Astrid's horse just eyes me sorrowfully as it to say, 'It was so cosy in the barn; and I think the grey horse in there has the hots for me.' But a hefty slap on the rump sends her trotting up the lane. I just hope Duke Solbakken will think his difficult son took off back to Oslo.

I feel no pity for Bertil. The Solbakken's son had been a murderer, a wolf, and he had been bitten by a wolf with much sharper teeth. But I do feel sorry for the family. In a week or two, they will return to Oslo and they will expect him to greet them. A little sourly, perhaps, but, still, they will expect him to be there.

I know I must tell them; tell them Bertil was a SWARM assassin and I had to kill him. Kill him and toss his body in a dry well.

The family will detest me for it and, undoubtedly, Duke Solbakken will challenge me to a duel of swords. But it is better they know. My thoughts echo Colonel Fiquet's words to me in France. There is nothing to be accomplished in them spending years watching the brass-knobbed, brass-knockered door for the boy's return.

I wonder, for a moment, if my mum and dad do just that; watch the warped and worm-ridden door in Jokkmokk for my return. But it hurts too much to brood over and I shrug the thought away.

Strolling back over to the Wily Wolf, I wipe the telltale

sawdust of my trousers and tunic. Then, stopping momentarily on the porch, I spot there is blood on my hands. I instantly throw up over a potted fern just by the door. Wiping my chin on my sleeve, I apologise profusely to the plant, hook a smile on my lips and walk in.

Friday, 18th September, 1870
1 Day to Assassination Day

1325 hours, Stockholm, Sweden

Blixt follows the Solbakken's cart up the street to the King's Castle. It feels odd to be back in Stockholm. I had visited when I was a child; my Uncle Olof had lived here and I remember how much I had loved the city, the old archways, the cobbled streets and the tiny ramshackle shops. They cosy up to the path, drippy triangular roofs shadowing the sun, selling silks, kilned pots and tiny clockwork toys.

I'm happy to see it is not much different now.

We trundle by a bakery and I wet my lips to the smell of the pastry, and then a butcher's shop, pigs dangling in the window. I spot old men rolling beer barrels and a boy rolling a hoop, his hair the colour of summer straw.

It is odd to be back, yes, but it feels good too.

The rest of the journey had been pretty uneventful. We had ridden through the tiny towns of Karlskog and Örebro and then in Köping, we had hopped on a ferry and taken it the rest of the way to Stockholm.

I had been unable to sleep properly on the trip, the men I lost in France never far from my thoughts. I see them on the backs of my eyelids, shadowy ghosts all twisted and bloody. Full of fury, they yell, 'WHY ME? WHY NOT THE MAN NEXT TO ME?' And now the boy, Bertil, is with them too.

Thankfully, the duke had swallowed my cock and bull story. I had told him I had witnessed his son pinch his sister's horse and gallop off in a rage. Luckily for me, the girl in the bar had slapped Bertil when he had attempted to kiss her, adding a spark of credibility to my shaggy dog tale.

In fact, the duke seemed almost happy to see the back of his son. Perhaps he had been scared Bertil might embarrass him at the party. I chuckle to myself. I guess stabbing the king of Sweden with a dagger would be a little embarrassing.

My job is over. I stopped the assassin and I'm now a hundred Danish kronor richer and the owner of the very

unique Tyrfing sword. So why don't I just say goodbye to the Solbakken family? Why do I feel so jumpy, I wonder. I chew on my bottom lip. The problem is the musket.

Bertil had been seventeen, maybe eighteen; too young to be an expert with both a knife and a rifle. Could there perhaps be a second assassin, a backup if Bertil missed the target? Do SWARM assassins work in twos, I ponder.

The Solbakken's cart judders up the cobbled street and into the courtyard of Sweden's royal castle. Like a bully in a schoolyard, it towers over the rest of Stockholm, a puzzle of brooding windows, carved lions and colossal marble pillars.

Drowsily, I clamber off Blixt and stretch. I feel horribly stiff and after two weeks of travelling there is cramp in my legs and I feel utterly spent.

I watch two of the king's butlers hurry over to help the Solbakkens to unpack. The duke is fussing over his beloved golf clubs and the duchess is still in the wagon, pruning herself with the help of a matching silver-handled mirror and brush. I look over to Astrid; she is chatting to the groom and helping him to unhitch the horse. I catch her eye and she slips me the shadow of a wink.

I decide, then and there, I'm being ridiculous. My job is over. The assassin is lying in a well with a dagger in his chest and the Swedish king is safe. Tomorrow, Prince Frederick of Denmark will be here for the party. Then, I will report my success to him and collect my pay.

I doubt I will see much of the Solbakkens now, so, wondering idly if Astrid will miss me, I stroll over to the old duchess to say my first goodbye. Offering her my hand, she accepts and steps off the wagon.

My jaw hits my chest, my mind reeling. How had I been so blind?

'Bless you, Major,' she thanks me. 'You got us here, well,' she smirks, 'most of us.'

I nod, lost for words.

I had just discovered there is a second assassin. But, most importantly, I had just discovered who it is.

1445 hours

A skinny girl with sandaled feet and anklets of silver bells shows me to my room in the castle.

It is tiny and had been furnished by a miserly hand: there is a bed, a bible, a wonky stool and a tapestry of Uppsala Cathedral on the mould-pitted wall. I thump the mattress and smile. After three years sleeping in tents, it feels sinfully soft.

There is a washroom too and a slim cupboard to put my tunic and boots in.

My window looks north past a crumbling bird's nest on the sill and over the busy Stockholm docks. I peer out to see hundreds of ships in port; sawmills and the waterwheels powering them; the royal stable and the opera house. Beyond is Arvfurstens Palace, a clock tower peeking over the top of the slate roof.

'I'll put fresh sheets on your bed,' tweets the girl, skipping over to the cupboard. She twirls on her heels. 'Two pillows or one?'

'Two,' I say. 'Let's be crazy.' Then, 'Tack.' Swedish for 'Thank you'.

When I had asked Duke Solbakken for his assistance in procuring a bed in the castle, he had been all too keen to help. In fact, a word from him topped with a copper penny and the thin-lipped butler had instantly handed me a key.

According to Astrid, her dad thinks I'm a 'very decent fellow'.

'Well, I am,' I had told her.

She had then asked me if I had ever given flowers to a woman. 'Absolutely not,' I had answered snootily. 'Why would I murder a perfectly good rose just to fulfil the romantic whims of a woman?' I then went on to ask her if she, for example, would be happy if on her birthday a man handed her a skewered hamster.

In retrospect, I think perhaps I need to work on my 'wooing' skills. But I still think my point was well made.

I drape my saddle bags over the stool. There's not much in them, just my box of inks and the book I draw my flowers in. I call it 'The Ramblings of a Swedish Botanist'. Sort of catchy, I think.

Then I turn to watch the girl unfold my sheets. 'My name is Tor,' I tell her. 'What's yours?'

'Gurli.'

Gurli has cherry-red curls, hazel eyes and a petal-blossoming smile. She also has a bump over her eye and I wonder how she got it.

'Snap,' I say, my finger hovering over my own blackened eye.

She looks to me, a wobbly smile hopping up on her lips. It promptly falls off. 'Snap,' she says sorrowfully.

I pull on the two week old whiskers on my chin, feeling sorry for her. She really is terribly skinny, her skin thin and papery, her dress draped over her body like a bell over a toothpick. But best not to meddle. 'Do you live here in the King's Castle?' I ask her.

Her mood lifts and she nods, tucking in the corners of my bed. 'Yes. We moved here from Malmö when Mum fell ill with dysentery and Father lost his job. I was only six, but I'm ten now,' she adds, proudly winching up her chin. 'Now Father works in the kitchen here; he's the pastry chef.'

'Wow! You must know every nook and cranny.'

A smile plays on her lips and her eyes dance. 'I do. Even the secret tunnels,' she adds, spiking my interest.

Storing this tasty morsel in the back of my mind, I return her smile. 'So, this big party of the king's is tomorrow?'

'Yes,' she fluffs up my two pillows, 'seven o'clock start. Everybody who's anybody will be there, Karl Marx, the author Fyodor Dostoyevsky. Oh, did I say it correctly? Even Alfred Nobel, the Swedish inventor. He's my hero. The king's in Uppsala hunting deer but he will be back in the morning.' I watch her bundle up the old sheets. 'There will be food in the scullery soon: fisk soppa.'

Fish soup! 'Underbart!' I miss Swedish cooking. 'Just let

118

me wash up.'

She hands me a towel and I stroll over to my washroom, shutting the door. My mind is full of the old duchess and the spider tattoo I had just seen on her wrist. So she must be the sniper, the backup if Bertil missed, and I'm betting the birthday party tomorrow is where she's planning to do the dastardly deed.

In the tiny room I find a sink and over it, a mirror. Reluctantly, I peer in it. The bump over my eye is now yellowy purple; but it is not the bump that is worrying me. Gingerly, I peel off the dressing on my cheek.

I swallow. 'Oh my,' I mumble. The cut is red and rawer than French cooked beef. It runs from the corner of my eye to the corner of my lips.

I look like a ruddy pirate.

Gingerly, I put my thumb to my cheek but a bolt of fire mushrooms from it and almost puts me to my knees. I hold on to the sink for a moment, fuzzy dots stabbing my eyes.

By the tap in a china pot is a kungsängslilja, or king's bed lily in English. The pink bell-shaped flower looks a little droopy so I water it, and, instantly, I feel better. Watering flowers truly is the best therapy in the world.

'GURLI! GET HERE NOW!' There is so much punch to

the words, they rock the door. Clomping footsteps, then, 'I told you to scrape the ovens, girl.'

'I forgot, Father. Sorry.'

'Then maybe my belt will help you to remember.'

'No, Father, no!'

I yank open the door to my room and discover a spindly, aproned man in there, his knee pressed to Gurli's chest, pinning her to the floor. In his hand is the threatened belt.

A wave of fury grips me and I grab his shoulder, pulling him off her. He swings a clumsy fist but I block it and thump him hard in the stomach. He drops to the floor, wheezing. It seems I must brawl ever cook I meet.

Yanking him to his knees, I pincer his cheeks in my fingers. 'To destroy a child's trust is a sin,' I snarl. 'If you hurt her, I will find you and then you'll wish you'd never been born. Got it?'

'Got it,' he whimpers.

'Then go and scrape your own ovens,' I seethe, pulling him to his feet and kicking him out of the door.

I turn to the girl and help her up. 'Did he hurt you, Sylva?'

'No, well, just my chest, but only a little.' She frowns. 'I'm er, Gurli by the way, not Sylva.'

'Oh! Yes, sorry.'

She looks to me, her eyes full of wonder, a love-struck puppy.

I feel my cheeks burn crimson and I mentally slap myself. I had been too rash and I ponder what her bully of a father will do to her when I ride off into the sunset.

'Th - thanks Tor,' she stammers. 'He's not so bad, you know. Not always. Just, well,' she rubs her eyes, 'I think he must miss Mum.'

'Punching you will not bring her back,' I tell her softly.

'I know, but, he's my dad.'

I nod, bowing to the simplicity of a child's mind. He's her dad.

Smiling, I sit her on the bed and kneel to look at her. 'I need your help,' I tell her frankly. 'The king's birthday tomorrow; I must see the room it will be held in.'

'The er, Vita havet?'

I nod.

'But nobody's supposed to go in there till the party. If anybody spots us...'

'Gurli,' I clasp her hand and gently squeeze her fingers, 'this is important.'

She scowls and absentmindedly thumbs the cleft of her chin. 'I suppose, but we can't go up the East Steps; everybody

will see us.' Then her lips curl up. 'But I know a different way.'

Hopping to my feet, I grab for my sword, buckling it to my hip.

'Now!? But, Tor, I thought you were hungry.'

I remember the box with the rifle still in it hooked to the belly of the Solbakken's wagon and my blood pumps. 'I prefer my fish soup cold,' I snap. 'Anyway, our job now is to stop a murderer.'

'A murderer!' she gasps.

I nod solemnly. Then I pop and fetch the kungsängslilja and put it on the window sill by the bird's nest.

'It needs a bit of sun,' I explain, feeling ever so slightly foolish.

1530 hours

Of all the rooms Gurli had just led me through, Vita havet is by far the most stunning. 'White Sea' in English, it is the size of a landowner's barn and has intricately decorated panelled walls and row upon row of arched windows. The wooden floor has been polished to a mirror and thirteen smooth pillars hold up a roof of sparkling chandeliers.

I see every nook and cranny has been stuffed with silvery tinsel and a butler is stood on a stepladder trying to drape a 'Gratulera På Födelsedagen' banner, or 'Happy Birthday', from one corner of the room to the other.

He eyeballs us coldly. 'Nobody's supposed to be in here,' he barks.

'Put a cork in it,' I retort sharply.

Pursing up his lips, he tuts and returns huffily to his banner.

With a dry mouth, I stroll by a punch bowl and a pyramid of goblets and over to a north-facing window, my footsteps echoing dully in the vast hall. My gaze is instantly met by Arvfurstens Palace and her labyrinth of darkened windows and shadowy roofs, all of them perfect for a sniper to hide in with a powerful musket.

I can see it now: King Karl XV thanking his guests for his birthday presents, a silver orb perhaps, or a flower from a far off land, when, suddenly, there is a shot, the window shatters…

I feel my fists curl and my blood run cold. I must find a way to stop Duchess Solbakken from shooting the Swedish king.

It is not just the sword, Tyrfing, and the hundred Danish kronor which fuels me now. I had seen too much blood spilt in France and much too much of it had been spilt by me. If it is in my power to stop a war, then I will stop it. Perhaps then, the ghosts of the men I lost will let me sleep.

Crossing the room, my eyes fall on the inner courtyard. It is chock-full of wagons now but I quickly spot the red wheels of the Solbakken's cart. The yard looks pretty much deserted except for a butler or two and the odd wild cat scavenging for scraps. But for my allergy to all things feline, now is the perfect opportunity for me to pinch the rifle. The duchess will find it pretty difficult to shoot the king if she has no weapon to do it with.

Twirling on my heel, I discover Gurli by my elbow. 'Vita havet is the third biggest room in the palace,' she tells me, 'after the church and the Hall of State, of course…'

'Gurli, I don't want to interrupt you, but I must get to the courtyard.'

She nods, beckoning me with her finger. 'Follow me. Oh, I can show you were Queen Sofia slept. She was Danish, you know, the wife of Gustav III…'

After dashing through Bernadotte gallery and Sofia Magdalena's bedchamber, and with a running commentary from Gurli of kings and queens and who killed who and who slept where, we exit the palace.

'Gurli, stay here.'

She nods, her cheeks flushed, her lips set to happy moon. 'I can be your look out.'

Gutsy. I smile and pinch her chin. She reminds me of my sister.

I scurry over to the parked wagons. There, I quickly spot the red wheels of the Solbakken's and I dash over to it. Glancing over my shoulder, I see two butlers enjoying a crafty vodka and a boy feeding potato peel to a stray tabby. I scratch involuntarily; by tomorrow my chest will probably be a mess of red spots.

Nobody seems to be looking my way, so I drop to a knee and peer under the wagon…

I wring my hands in helplessness. The tiny coffin is nowhere to be seen.

1745 hours

Two hours later, I sit in the scullery and sup on a bowl of cold watery kipper soup. It is very tidy in here. Every stool, I see,

every pot and every pan, looks old and badly worn, but there's not a spot of dirt. No dust trolls in the corners, no cobwebs on the potter's wheel. The cook must be a dragon to work for. A stiff-backed iron sits on the hob and idly ponders if and when to attack a crumpled hill of tunics in a wicker basket on the floor, and a rack of cow's ribs hooked to the rafters seeps blood in the sink.

I find the 'Drip! Drip! Drip!' a little unnerving.

There is nobody here but me, oh, and the annoyingly chirpy cuckoo in the pendulum clock over the door. It seems, according to the squinty-eyed butler I met, everybody is up in Vita havet blowing up balloons and unboxing rockets for the birthday party tomorrow.

Even Gurli slipped off, but I think she's scraping her dad's ovens in the kitchen up on the second floor.

My mind is a whirling twirling tornado of whens, wheres, whos and hows. The musket, I ponder, must be in the duchess's bedchamber. My plan: to slip in there and try to find it; destroy it if I must. The problem: how to do it and not be spotted by any member of the Solbakken family?

There is a knock and I look up from my soup. The scullery door swings open and to my joy, Astrid strolls in, her feet swirling up her linen dress. I had only ever seen her in

126

jodhpurs and I must say, she looks very pretty.

I try not to drool.

Gentlemanly, I hop to my feet. 'Hello there!' I cry.

'Hi.' She looks a little bemused by the warmth of my welcome. 'I thought I'd just pop and say goodbye.'

'Oh!' I feel my shoulders slump; I had hoped to enjoy a romantic 'hand in hand' stroll with her in the city. 'Off on your travels, hey?' I rally, in a poor attempt at nonchalance. 'Where to? Back to Oslo? Do you miss your hamster?'

'Hamster!?' She shudders. 'They remind me of rats.'

I frown. How odd! I remember the Solbakken's family butler told me...

'Anyway, I'm not 'off' anywhere.' She pulls up a stool and sits. I sit too. 'But I thought, you know, with the birthday party only tomorrow...'

'Oh, yes.' I thump my brow with my hand. 'Gripenstedt.' The ferrety lord had slipped my mind.

'Anyway, I think the French need you back. Word is,' she drops to a whisper; a secret to be told, 'Paris will fall to the Germans any day now.'

'Not my war,' I tell her bluntly. Too bluntly and I instantly regret it. Ponderously, I stir my broth. 'Look, the ruddy Germans killed every trooper in my regiment; a hundred and

twenty-three men. I was their commanding officer; they trusted me and now, well,' I swallow, 'now there's nobody left for me to command.'

'I'm sorry.'

I nod and poke at a bobbing kipper eye. 'So am I,' I mutter. Then I wave my spoon at a pot on the hob by the iron. 'There's fish broth over there if you fancy a bowl.'

She looks over to the corner of the scullery. 'Tempting, but I'd better not.' Her eyes cut to the sink and the bloody lump of beef hooked over it. She licks her lips wistfully. 'My family's been invited to supper with the Queen. Grilled lobster, I think, with shrimp. Oh, and a rhubarb crumble.'

I nod understandingly. Cold kippers with a mercenary will never win over lobsters and rhubarb crumble with a Swedish queen.

'Actually, I'd much prefer to be here with you, but duty calls.'

I almost drop my spoon. A bull is stampeding in my chest. She prefers it here with me and a bowl of smelly kippers than with the Queen of Sweden enjoying a lobster supper. I sip broth and try not to dribble on my chin.

'Tell me, Tor, what do you plan to do now? Your job here is over. You got the Solbakkens to Stockholm...'

'Most of them,' I interrupt her.

Her lips curl up. 'Yes.' She nods. 'Most of them.'

It dawns on me, a little uncomfortably, that I have not yet told her, or any of the Solbakken family, of Bertil's watery fate. But if I do, I know Astrid will detest me for it. He was her brother, after all. If I'm honest, this is why I do not tell them and not the prospect of duelling a grief-stricken father.

'You seem awfully keen to be rid of me,' I say to her, keen to steer the talk away from such shark-infested waters. Or wells.

'NO! No.' She shows me her palms. 'Honestly, I'm not. I just worry. I'd hate for this Gripenstedt-fellow to spot you.'

I relent and drop my spoon in my bowl. 'If you must know, I thought maybe I'd go on holiday.' I watch her closely. 'Oslo perhaps. If you want to; if you, you know, happen to be there, you can show me the city.'

I rest my hands on the table in a pathetic attempt to stop them from trembling. Unfortunately, my elbow knocks the stem of my spoon and it flips up, showering me with sticky broth and dropping a kipper's eyeball on my lap.

I decide to play it cool so, nonchalantly, I pop the errant eyeball in my mouth as if to say, 'It so happens this is the way I always enjoy my food.'

Astrid jumps to her feet, almost tipping over her stool. For a split second, I wonder did a spider or a rat just scamper over her foot. 'I'd er, better be off,' she blusters. 'Supper's at nine o'clock and now it's, er...' She looks wildly over her shoulder to the clock on the wall.

'Almost six,' I tell her coldly, wiping my cheek on my sleeve. Perhaps she mistakenly thinks I just asked her to murder her fluffy hamster; a hamster she mysteriously cannot remember.

'Yes! Yes! Six o'clock. Only three hours till lobster.' She fills the scullery with a jittery chuckle and backs over to the door. 'My, my, so much to do. I must find my jewellery, put on my best dress...'

I pick my spoon up off the floor. 'Yes, a dress can be awfully difficult to put on,' I murmur scornfully to the underbelly of the table.

'It can be,' she spits, catching my words.

'If you plan to knit it first,' I spit back, 'and then sew on the buttons.'

Ruthlessly, I watch her hop from foot to foot. Let her suffer. 'The problem is, Major Tor...'

Oh, it's MAJOR Tor now. 'Just forget it,' I snap. 'I understand. The daughter of a rich duke and a poor mercenary; hardly the perfect match.'

'NO! No.' She stops hopping and begins to rock on her heels. 'Well, maybe, perhaps, but,' now she's rubbing her temple too, 'look, I'm very complicated...'

'So is cheese,' I blurt out.

She scowls, not getting it. Nor do I but I plough on anyway. 'Well, the farmer, you know, he's got to milk the cow, then er, blend it - the milk,' I add hastily, 'not the cow. Then there's the er...' I stop and chew on my lip. I'm a jabbering idiot. Why is it, whenever I talk to this woman, my mind seems to disconnect from my vocal cords?

Astrid cocks her head bemusedly. I think she thinks I'm a fool, but, perhaps, if I'm lucky, a terribly sweet fool. 'Tor, can I offer you a tiny bit of advice?'

I nod. Anything if it will stop my cheese babbling.

'Get out of Sweden,' she tells me brutally. 'Not tomorrow, not a week on Thursday. Now! This very moment.' She puts her hands on her hips. 'Until then, try not to do anything - stupid.'

'So you think I'm stupid,' I bark, jutting out my jaw.

'No, Tor, I think your cheese speech was stupid. Foolhardy is a much better word for you.'

'Hey, I don't hunt for trouble.' Then, ruefully, I mutter, 'It

just sort of seems to find me.'

For a second, the yellow tint in her eyes swells, smoothing her pupils. It is a remarkably odd phenomenon. 'Goodbye Tor,' she says softly. 'Whenever I see tulips I will always think of my chaperon to Sweden.'

The door clunks shut hiding her flapping heels. I sit there, a scowl crumpling my brow, hypnotised by the clock's pendulum. I think Astrid thinks I plan to duel Lord Gripenstedt. That or start up a cheese factory.

Snatching up my spoon, I return to my bowl of soup. I feel limp; flattened hay in the summer storms.

Why is it I remind her of a pretty little flower, I wonder crossly, and not a bull or a bold musketeer, his sword clutched in his ivory-knuckled fist. A prickly cactus even. But, oh no, I remind her of a ruddy tulip!

'Women,' I mutter sourly. To me they seem a total and utter mystery; all whim-wham and fribble-frabble.

The cuckoo pops out of the clock and chirrups joyfully at me. I respond by tossing my bowl of soup at it.

2135 hours

'Here is it,' whispers Gurli, scampering up the corridor and handing me a bronze key. 'It fits every lock in the castle; even the King's bedchamber.'

'Superb,' I mutter. I hold it up to study it. 'Where did you find it?'

'On Johan, the old porter. Friday is his day off and he always drinks three tumblers of vodka and falls asleep in the scullery. I snatched it off his belt.'

I nod admiringly and pinch her cheek to thank her.

With our footsteps muffled by a deep woollen carpet, we skulk up the corridor and by a marble bust of a bug-eyed, banana-nosed queen.

'Hedvig Eleonora of Holstein-Gottorp,' Gurli tutors me.

'Gigantic hooter,' I comment dryly.

'Runs in the family.' Then she titters. 'Get it? Her nose. It runs. In the family.'

Mustering a chuckle, I pull her after me until, finally, and thankfully with no further 'nose' gags, I feel a sharp jerk on my tunic sleeve. 'This is it,' says Gurli. 'On the 13th March, 1809, Swedish officers met in this room to plan the overthrow of Gustav IV Adolf.'

'But how do you know Duke and Duchess Solbakken sleep here?'

'The butler; he told me. He sent me to put fresh blankets on the bed and to empty the vase by the window. Oh!' She looks sheepishly to her feet and rubs her chin. 'The flowers!'

I squeeze her elbow and tell her not to worry. Then I creep over to the door and slip the key in the lock. 'Let's hope they enjoy the lobster and stay for seconds,' I whisper over my shoulder.

'Dessert too,' my partner in crime mutters back.

I nod, and, with trembling fingers, I twist the magic key and put my shoulder to the wood.

The Solbakkens had helpfully left a lamp burning on a French dresser and I instantly see the room is empty. I feel my shoulders relax and I stroll in, Gurli on my heels.

It is a corner room, lavishly decorated with flowery wallpaper, antique mirrors and a crystal chandelier. The dresser is on sentry duty by the door and in the very middle of the room there is a colossal four-poster bed. On it, I spy Duke Solbakken's golf clubs.

'So, my job's to look for a musket.' Gurli eyes the room with deep ferocity as if to suggest it surrender now and hand the gun over.

134

'Yes,' I reply. I spy a vase on the window sill with a few limp sprigs of rowanberry in it and I chuckle. The butler will not be happy. Then I recall there had been no powder and shot in the coffin under the Solbakken's cart. 'Oh, and look for a box of tiny iron balls too,' I add, 'and black powder.'

Gurli nods and skips over to the French dresser. She pulls open the top drawer. I, on the other hand, trot over to the clubs on the bed. But all I discover is a pocket full of balls and three clubs: a pitcher, a driver and a putter. For a man who seems so keen on the sport they look very shiny and new and there is hardly a scratch on the balls.

I look up and my eyes cut to Gurli. She is still by the French dresser; I see the second from top drawer is now open and I spy a tiny yellow bottle in her hand.

A shadow of worry knots my brow and my eyes narrow. 'What is it?' I ask her. 'Perfume?'

'Lemon, by the looks of it.' Uncorking the bottle, she puts it to her lips.

'NO!' I cry.

I drop the club back on the bed and hurry over to her, snatching the bottle from her fingers. Then I sniff it; just a whiff but instantly I know what it is, my mind swamped with a memory of my mum and I in the kitchen in Jokkmokk; she's

showing me how to gut and skin a particularly ugly fish.

Horror crawls over my skin; throbs in my chest. If Gurli had even sipped it…

'I discovered it hidden under a jumper in a sock.' She shows me the sock; it is pink with tiny yellow snowmen on it.

Duke Solbakken's sock! I remember the butler in Oslo telling the duke he had packed them for him.

Thoughtfully, I stopper the bottle and hand it back over to Gurli. 'Do me a favour, run to the kitchen and swap what's in there with squeezed lemon.'

She holds it up to the lamp. 'Shall I tip this down the sink?'

'No. Put it in a different bottle. Oh,' I clutch her shoulder, 'and remember to wash your hands - thoroughly,' I add with a stern fatherly look.

She nods and dutifully, she skips over to the door.

'Lock it after you,' I tell her, 'and keep the key in your pocket.'

She departs the Solbakken's bedchamber with a sunny, if not slightly puzzled smile, and a second later the key twists in the lock. I turn to the room, my fists on my hips. Now, where had this clever assassin hidden the musket?

I hunt everywhere: in, under and on top of the wardrobe, down the back of the dresser, even under the iron bathtub, but the rifle stays stubbornly hidden.

Crawling under the bed to look, I hear a key in the lock.

Gurli! She has the speed of a cheetah.

I watch the bottom of the door open, but it is not Gurli's anklets of silver bells I see; it is the perfectly sewn hem of a velvety, daffodil-yellow dress.

Hidden under the bed, I crunch my knees up to my chin. It must be Duchess Solbakken.

I listen to her lock the door and the key clunk onto the French dresser. Then I watch her kick off her slippers and hurry over to the balcony door.

The balcony! Mentally, I hit my brow with my hand. I had not thought to look there.

I catch the rasp of a bolt being drawn back, but, just then, the door to the room is unlocked and two smaller, slightly paler feet jingle in.

OH NO! Gurli!

The duchess's feet scamper back over to the bed and, all of a sudden, the wooden planks under the mattress bow and almost crush my skull to the floor.

'Is it not custom to knock in Sweden?' I hear her bark.

'Oh, sorry, Duchess Solbakken. The er, butler sent me up to put fresh flowers in your vase.'

Good recovery, I think.

'I see,' she snaps. 'Well, they do look a little droopy.'

'Yes. Yes, they do. If the Queen sees them she'll be very upset. She insists on newly cut flowers in every room.'

Cautiously, I peer out from under the bed. Gurli spots me and I jab my thumb at the dresser.

She rewards me with two blinks and a tiny, tiny nod.

I slip back under the bed and watch her feet scurry over to the window where I remember seeing the vase with the limp rowanberry in it, sitting on the sill.

'I was told you were enjoying a lobster supper with the queen,' Gurli tells the duchess. 'Which is why I did not knock.'

'Yes, well, I was but I er, felt terribly ill. Poorly tummy. It is better I rest for the birthday party tomorrow; I do not want to miss it.'

'Oh my! Can I help? If you wish me to I can pull the drape over your bed. It will help to keep you warm.'

Clever. She's button smart this girl.

'Yes. Yes, why not?' murmurs the duchess with a lilt of martyrdom. 'If it will help.'

I catch the swish of velvet, then, 'There. Much better,' Gurli tells her.

Indeed it is. The duchess is now hidden from the room and, most importantly, the room is hidden from the duchess. Now there's no way she will see me when I try to exit.

I peer up at Gurli and watch her hurry over to the dresser, softly inch open the second from top drawer and slip the bottle back in the sock. A bottle full of squeezed lemon, I hope.

She twirls on her heel and drops to a knee. 'Now,' she mouths to me.

'No,' I mouth back, jabbing my thumb at the door. 'Go!' I will her to understand. I must try to find the musket.

'But...' she begins to whisper.

'Be off with you!' booms the duchess from her bed.

Gurli jumps to her feet. 'Sorry, Duchess, I er, spilt water on the carpet.' She shoots me a cheeky wink. 'I mopped it up; it will soon dry. I will return shortly with fresh flowers.'

'Do it tomorrow, Girl,' insist the duchess. She yawns ostensively. 'I need my sleep and do not wish to be disturbed.'

'Yes, Madam.' Then she whispers, 'Good luck' to me and slips from the room.

Quietly, I crawl out from under the bed and over to the balcony, the only part of the room I have not yet explored. I

see Duchess Solbakken left the door unbolted and slightly ajar so, still on my knees, I slip out.

Scrambling to my feet, I instantly know the musket is not here. For a start, the balcony is only six foot by three, bordered by the twirly limbs of a wind-sanded iron balustrade. It is also almost barren; there is only a limp Arctic poppy in a beehive-shaped pot in the corner and the skeletal body of a bird, a jay by the look of it, by my boot. There is simply nowhere to hide it.

Dismayed, I turn back to the door. It is still ajar and instantly I spot the drape on the assassin's bed has been pulled up and hooked back on the canopy.

But Duchess Solbakken is no longer in her bed.

With my cowardly knees knocking up a drum roll, I put my eye to the crack. I instantly spy her over by the French dresser. Her back is to me but she looks to be fiddling with the lantern there.

I don't know exactly why, but I find this plump, fifty year old woman terribly scary. Perhaps it is her cold eyes or her jaw of tomb-black teeth. Or perhaps it is the fact that she hardly ever says a word but I can still tell she feverently detests me.

Suddenly, she twists on her heels and I bunny-hop back

from the door.

I must hide!

But if there's nowhere to hide a musket, then there's nowhere to hide a man.

I see there is a second balcony level to Duchess Solbakken's. Quickly, I clamber over the top of the balustrade, bend my knees and with the Lord's Prayer on my lips, I jump. I hit the other balustrade so hard I almost ricochet off. I plummet, my clawing fingers catching on the bottom rung.

I hang there, a pig in a butcher's shop soon to be slaughtered.

Peering up and over my shoulder, I spot the duchess on her balcony. Oddly, she is waving her lantern to and fro; she sort of reminds me of a signalman trying to stop a runaway locomotive.

I feel my hands begin to cramp and I twist back, my eyes fixed determinedly on the moon and not on the fifty foot drop to the stone-slabbed footway.

The seconds tick slowly by.

Soon, I know, the assassin will look over and see me. Or I will fall and shatter every bone in my body.

I must hold on. I MUST!

Presently, I catch the plod of footsteps and the welcome thump of her balcony door.

With the fervour of a burrowing rodent, I claw my way up and over the balustrade. I drop to the floor and for a second I lay starfished on the cold iron. I must be crazy. All this for a hundred Danish kronor and a shiny sword. But all too soon my mind prods me to my feet with thoughts of Duchess Solbakken and what she had been up to with the lantern.

Tiredly, I peer over the balcony to the docks below. But all I can see of interest is the opera house - it is lit up; there must be a show on - and the gloomy silhouette of a ship. There is a lantern on the bow and I can just see the words 'Goyo-Goyuku' embossed on her hull. She reminds me very much of an upturned bathtub but if I remember correctly from my dad's History of Ships, she must be an old ironclad from the American Civil War.

I wonder, idly, why she is here in Sweden.

There is no way I will risk the jump back over to Duchess Solbakken's balcony, so I try the door on this balcony and, mercifully, it is unbolted.

Immediately, a deafening growl assaults my ears. There is a man in there, presumably asleep on the bed. With such a thunderous snore, I doubt even if I tripped over and fell on

him he'd wake up.

Confidently, I stroll over to the far door.

A dying candle on a stool flickers, throwing a yellow sheen over the fellow's face.

My boots catch the carpet and I almost stumble. Suddenly, there is a drummer in my skull; a trumpeter too. The volcano in me stirs, the molten lava trapped by only a thin crust of skin and willpower.

The man on the bed is Lord Gripenstedt, my mortal enemy.

I pull my sword and trip dazedly over to him. Then, ruthlessly, I put the blade to his sallow cheek. He looks so much older than I remember; feeble even, his skin yellowy and speckled with liver spots. But this man destroyed my life; forced me to flee my home and desert my family. Just a tiny jab and I can return to them.

I swallow and, sternly, I order my hand to pull the sword away from his cheek. Hesitantly, it obeys me. His son, Christoffer, had murdered my sister but I, in return, had murdered his son. In cold blood. Astrid had been spot on. It had hardly been the worthy act of a musketeer. And I doubt my soul will survive if I do it for a second time.

With rock-filled boots, I slump over to the door. Thankfully, it is unlocked and I slip out, Lord Gripenstedt's thunderous snore almost propelling me from the room. I balloon my cheeks and allow the door to click shut after me. If only my petty sorrows allowed me to sleep so deeply.

Saturday, 19th September, 1870
Assassination Day

1655 hours, the King's Palace, Stockholm

I sit on my stool by my bedroom window and study the kungsängslilja on the sill. It is a truly wonderful flower, to a botanist anyway. Carl Von Linné, Sweden's celebrated expert on plants, had thought it grew only in Uppsala, just north of Stockholm. I now know he was mistaken. Two weeks ago, I had seen a nest of them in the flower beds of Denmark's Royal Palace.

I sniff it and catch the sweet smell of honey in my nostrils.

But Linné was often mistaken; I remember he also attempted to classify rocks by sex. Boy rocks! Oddly stupid for such a clever fellow.

By my feet is the bottle Gurli discovered in the Solbakken's bedchamber and my wooden box of pencils, pens and ink pots. The pots sit in two rows of four on red velvety cloth, a present, sent to me by my Grandmother Toyi in China for my 18th birthday. I never met her but she often sent letters to my mum and I know she enjoy a spot of botany too. She even had 'TOR' etched on the lid, a poppy climbing the trunk of the 'T'.

I pick up a pencil and with the sweep of my hand, the wavy stem is drawn. I find this is the best way to do it; it is important the stem flows and is not jerky or bumpy. The top of the stem, I see, bows over to the bell-shaped flower. Charily, I sketch the border of the petal and pepper it with dots.

I had been shocked yesterday to see Lord Gripenstedt, my enemy and the father of my sister's murderer, asleep on the bed. I mostly blame his son for what happened, but I blame him too. Is it not a father's job to instil in his children a little decency? Do they not say, the apple never falls far from the tree?

In my mind he is a monster too.

But when I spotted him there in his woolly pyjamas and innocuous tartan slippers, I thought only of a grandpa enjoying a nap after pruning his flowerbeds.

No third eye, no wolf's teeth. In fact, not a monster at all.

My sketch is now in need of a little colour. I unstopper the ink pots and dib my pen's tiny copper nib in the pink. Soon Lord Gripenstedt is blanketed with much sweeter thoughts of lilacy petals topped in emerald-jade, and yellow violet-spotted stems. Even the ever-present throb of my cut cheek is forgotten.

Presently, all I can think of is the kungsängslilja.

I feel happy.

Content.

I always enjoy being on my own. When I was a child growing up in Jokkmokk, the other boys in school played brännboll, a sport with a ball and a bat, and lots of players. I, however, much preferred chess, but only if my opponent was me. I even skipped Elof Alsvik's birthday party to hunt for chanterelle mushrooms on Padjelanta path, and, when I was seven, I dug a hole in the forest, just by a silver birch tree. Then, two weeks later, I filled it back in.

I still don't know why I dug the hole but it was wonderful fun. Just me and the worms, and a host of very happy birds.

Two hours slip by. It is September, so soon, I know, the sun will drop off the horizon and the flower's colours will be

lost to the dusk. Reluctantly, I stopper the ink pots, dry off the pens and put the book on the pillow to dry. I swap my wooden pencil for my wooden rifle, plonk my elbows on the window sill and look over to the rooftops of Arvfurstens Palace.

Now, where is she, I wonder.

1950 hours

A half hour later, I'm still sitting on my stool by my bedroom window, my rifle snoozing in my lap, the kungsängslilja snoozing by my feet. Well, I do not want to risk my elbow knocking it off the sill. It is dark now but the moon is three-quarter full, casting lazy shadows over the rooftops in front of me. I clench my jaw, my eyes hard. Shooting a lady in cold blood, even a lady intent on assassinating the Swedish monarch, sits uncomfortably in my stomach. I'm a trooper, a man of honour, d'Artagnan not the evil Count Richelieu. But I know if I let her murder King Karl, there may be a war and after the bloody butcher's shop of France I'm determined not to let that happen.

The king had promptly returned from his shoot in Uppsala

at eight o'clock that morning in the company of a wagon brimming with deer, and now, almost twelve hours later, his birthday party is in full swing. Two floors up, the orchestra is playing a Straus waltz and every so often I watch a pony and trap drop off a fresh batch of peacock-costumed nobility.

I look past the bird's nest to the palace, my eyes hunting the shadows for my target. But so far, nothing, only cats; hundreds of them, sleeping in the gutters or climbing the chimneys.

Ruddy toms. I clench my teeth, wondering where the duchess is and trying not to scratch the welts on my chest.

Suddenly, a fat ginger scampers over the palace roof. Scowling, I level my rifle, wondering what, or who had scared it, but my scope stays stubbornly empty.

I remember the duke told me he planned to hand his gift to the king at eight o'clock. Then, everybody will be there watching. Hmm. The perfect moment to shoot a bullet wrapped in a bow; a final present from Norway to Sweden, courtesy of the Solbakken family and the catalyst for war.

I risk a look to the clock on the church roof: 7.59, only a minute to go.

But the rooftop of Arvfurstens Palace is still utterly deserted. No sniper.

Puzzled, I rub my eyes. The palace is the only high up spot I can see, well, apart from the clock tower, but that must be four hundred and fifty yards away. Much too far…

Or is it…?

My mind ricochets back to the rifle I had discovered under the Solbakken's cart. The barrel had been so bulky, the scope so…

POWERFUL!

BONG!

With the church clock announcing eight o'clock to the city of Stockholm, I swing my musket.

There! Just by the swinging bell, the shiny barrel of a rifle. The rifle. Even from here it looks a monster.

The moon slips the motherly hug of a cloud and falls on the cheek of the shooter. I swallow. It's as if a bucket of icy water has been thrown over me and I almost drop my musket.

It cannot be.

IT CANNOT BE!

I waver, my finger flatly refusing to rest on the trigger. But if I allow her to shoot, she will be murdering the Swedish king and there will be war.

I remember Jasper, Pedro, all of my men lost to the mud of France. War is hell. 'Sorry,' I mutter and I pull the trigger.

My rifle, the only child of the best gunsmith in London, jerks in my grip.

The shot, I know, is good.

Dropping my musket to the floor, I just sit there, letting the wave of shock roll over me. I had just shot Astrid; intelligent, sweet, wonderful Astrid and I feel a fist of regret punch me in the belly. Saliva floods my mouth and I work hard not to throw up over the potted flower by my boot.

No wonder I had not succeeded in finding the musket when I ransacked Duchess Solbakken's bedchamber. It had been hidden in her daughter's room.

I thought the son was the assassin, and he had been, but so is the old duchess: I had seen her spider tattoo. And now, it seems, so was the daughter. The duke, I'm guessing, must be in on the plan too.

I feel for the rabbit's foot in my pocket. It is mind boggling. How can this organisation, SWARM, be so powerful it can corrupt every member of this old aristocratic family? And which of them, I wonder, is, or was, the wicked Locust?

I shake myself, a dog throwing off water. Then I snatch up the Solbakken's bottle and jump to my feet, my hand instinctively on my sword. I must find Duke Solbakken and

stop him. I must find Duchess Solbakken and stop her.

I must get to the party.

2015 hours, Vita havet

The last Swedish king to be assassinated was Gustav III in 1792, almost a hundred years ago, so, not surprisingly, security for Karl XV's birthday party is pretty poor.

Bypassing two corporals on sentry duty by the door, I slip in Vita havet by way of the kitchen. Nobody sees me, and, to be perfectly honest, nobody seems particularly interested, the twenty or so chefs way too busy baking tarts and whisking jordgubbssylt, a sort of strawberry jam. I spot Gurli's father too, slapping whipped butter-icing on the seventh tier of a twelve-tier cake.

All the men, but for me, look dapper and well-groomed in lofty top hats and wide-lapelled, deep-cuffed velvet jackets. My uniform is woollen, there is blood on my trousers and my tunic pocket's been ripped off. The women too look terribly chic; hundreds of bell-shaped gowns embellished with buttons and bows, frills and lacy ribbons. They remind me uncomfortably of my chat with Astrid in the scullery.

Perhaps, then, I had been mistaken. Perhaps a dress is very cumbersome to put on.

Trying not to step on too many silk slippers, I push my way through the crowd till, finally, I find a comfy marble column to rest my shoulder on.

The monocled king, I must say, looks very kingly, from the cluster of medals on his chest to the silver-tipped cane in his yellow-gloved hand. He is tall too, and chunky, perfect for lording over his lowly subjects.

By his elbow is Queen Lovisa. She is paler than chalk and has the gloomy look of an underfed basset hound.

She is watching her husband deliver his birthday speech, his noble guests lapping up his silvery words.

'Sweden and Norway, two lands united by common goals,' the king is saying in his deep tenor, but I pay him little heed; I'm too busy watching the duke by his other elbow. He looks awfully jumpy, like a poodle in a thunderstorm, undoubtedly wondering why his daughter, Astrid, has not put a bullet in the king's skull. 'Many of you lords here today only see Sweden, the doting father and Norway, the silly wayward child...'

The crowd titters, wondering, perhaps, if he is joking or not.

'…but I tell you now, this is a foolish way to think.'

The titters abruptly stop.

'Norway is not a conquest, it is a partner and Duke Solbakken and his good wife...' Karl looks to the duke and scowls, his monocle promptly popping out. 'By the way, where is the duchess?'

'She's er, unwell,' stutters the duke. 'Just a cold, I think. She's in bed, sleeping.'

'The poor woman felt terribly poorly yesterday,' pips in the queen. 'I think the lobster upset her.'

Her husband frowns. Perhaps he is not au fait with yesterday's supper menu and thinks the duchess had a row with a shellfish. 'Well, er, let's hope she is better soon. Now, where was I, oh yes, Duke Solbakken has travelled from Oslo to honour his king and strengthen the bonds between our two lands. We welcome him.'

There is a muted cheer and everybody claps. Not a 'we won the cup' sort of clap, but still, they clap.

'A toast to Sweden and Norway,' decrees the king. He stops to cough and a pencil-lipped butler hastens over to fill his goblet. 'May we grow ever stronger and ever closer.'

Goblets clink.

With interest, I watch the good duke put his cup to his lips to drink but his Adam's apple is still. The sly devil is not swallowing.

'The best part of any birthday party is unwrapping the presents.' Wiping punch off his chin, Karl slaps Solbakken's shoulder and pops his monocle back in. 'Let's see what Norway has for me.'

The duke nods enthusiastically, but I spot a look of puzzlement shadowing his eyes and I feel my own spirits lift.

The king picks up a pink-ribboned box, a hubbub of chatter rippling through the crowd of onlookers.

'I hope there's no bomb in here,' he titters cheerily, a tiny shadow of doubt in his twitchy nostrils. He looks up. 'Alfred!'

'The box is too small,' says the man by my elbow. So, this must be Alfred Nobel, the inventor and Gurli's hero. I look to him with interest. He has the hollow eyes of a man who enjoys very little sleep and the thick bushy eyebrows of a man who has no interest in trimming them.

'Excellent!' The king winks at the duke. 'Just joking, Old Fellow.'

The duke musters a tense smile, scratching his brow.

With the enthusiasm of a child on Christmas morning, Karl rips off the paper, and for a nasty second I wonder if Alfred

Nobel's mistaken and I almost shout to the king to stop. But, thankfully, the only thing to explode IS the king. In delight.

'How wonderful!' he howls. 'A set of pistols.'

'Gold pistols,' the duke corrects him. 'Set with emeralds.' He is now shuffling from foot to foot and looking very jittery.

'Sire, I forgot your second gift,' Solbakken suddenly blurts out. 'It is in my bedchamber but I shall fetch it for you. Do excuse me.'

But the king is too engrossed unwrapping his other presents and simply nods.

Duke Solbakken bows and slips away.

I almost lose him in the crowd, but I know exactly where he is off to, and it is not to his bedchamber. Discreetly, I follow him over to the punchbowl and, with satisfaction, I watch him snatch up the silver spoon and warily sniff it.

'Lemon juice,' I say, marching over to him.

Startled, he drops the spoon back in the punch and looks up. 'Major Tor,' now he remembers me, 'I, er…'

'You can smell lemon juice, Duke Solbakken.'

He titters hollowly, as if I'd just told a joke that turned out not to be funny at all. 'Been on the vodka, Old Fellow?' he mutters. He looks as if he just swallowed a chilli and he looks to his feet for help.

'I had a rummage in your bedchamber and I discovered this in your sock.' I pull a tiny bottle from my hip pocket. 'Blowfish venom. You see, my mum's Chinese and she showed me how to cook blowfish and not kill anybody. I still remember the smell. Anyway, I switched it for lemon juice and that is what you put in the punch. Oh, by the way, your sniper, Astrid, is sleeping. Forever!'

He eyeballs me coldly, his lips twisting in a snarl of hate.

'What, no 'Excellent! Excellent!'?' I taunt him, parodying his girlish soprano. 'Now tell me,' I step up to him, my hand resting threateningly on my sword, 'where can I find your good wife, the duchess?'

His eyes spark and surprisingly I see victory there. 'SWARM is everywhere. It will gobble you up and spit you out.'

Suddenly, he grabs the venom from my hand, pulls the cork and with a thirsty gulp, swallows the lot.

Stunned and numb with horror, I watch him topple over, thudding to the floor. 'Get a doctor,' I yell to the crowd, dropping to my knee.

Gently, I unbutton his collar. 'Who is the boss of SWARM?' I quiz him urgently. 'Where can I find him?'

'The web of a spider will always catch the fly,' he rasps

cryptically. He holds my eyes. I expect to see abhorrence in them - I did kill his daughter - but I see only pity. 'Mr Spider will find you, Major. There is no city, no town, no tiny hamlet you can hide in. He is not born of Eve and he knows your face now.'

A scowl furrows my brow. 'I met him! When?' Desperately, I grip the lapels of his tunic, ignoring the concerned gasps of the onlookers. 'TELL ME!' I cry.

But there is a far off look in his eyes. 'I played the role of the absentminded duke so very well, I thought.'

My jaw slackens. This is not Duke Solbakken. I swallow. 'Yes, you did,' I relent. Why not? The man is dying.

'But Prince Frederick plays poker with the duke, not chess. I got mixed up, you see; and his rings did not fit me properly and kept slipping off.' He is mumbling almost incoherently now, his body limp and splayed like a raggedy doll's. 'But I thought I did awfully well to disarm the highwayman. I often play the role of Macbeth so I'm very talented with a sword.'

Who is this man, I wonder.

'You know,' I frown, trying to catch his words, 'I may not be the most successful assassin in the world but by Prospero's tempest, I can act.'

Cramps rake his body and he grunts in agony, clenching

his teeth. 'There's blood on my hands,' he mutters. 'Out damned spot! Out, I say!' Then his eyelids flutter and his jaw slackens.

Feeling numb, I drag myself to my feet and begin to push my way through the jabbering crowd.

'Where's Duke Solbakken with my second present?' I hear the king shout.

I know Bertil had been an assassin, his plan I presume, to stab the Swedish king, and I now know Astrid had been his back up if he missed the target. But Duke Solbakken, who it now seems was not Duke Solbakken at all, had planned to put blowfish venom in the punch and to kill everybody at the party, not just Karl XV. If his wife, the duchess, is his back up, had she also a plan to murder everybody, and, if so, what is it?

I spy Alfred Nobel in the crowd and the cogs in my mind begin to turn. Looking to the floor, I suddenly remember what Gurli had told me, yesterday, in my room: 'I know all the secret tunnels too.'

'TOR!' I look up to find myself eye to eye with a lord; a lord I remember all too well. Gripenstedt! Unfortunately, he remembers me too. 'You murdered my son,' he howls.

I grip the lapel of his tunic. 'Your son murdered my sister,'

I spit back. Then I thump him on the chin.

With a startled cry, he cartwheels back, tripping over and…

But there's no time to stop and see him hit the floor. I hurry over to the kitchen, the word, 'VAKTER!', Swedish for 'GUARDS!' chasing my heels.

Shouldering open the door, my eyes wildly hunt the pots and pans and glowing ovens till I spot Gurli's father. There! Over by the pantry. I march up to him but he sees me and attempts to scarper, but my boot finds his scampering feet and I trip him up. I yank him off his knees and, not so gently, pin him to the wall.

'Tell me where Gurli is,' I command him.

Puckering up his lips, he glowers at me obstinately.

'So be it.' With my eyes blazing, I tow him over to the ovens. 'Tell me,' I cry, booting open the red hot door, 'or burn.'

He picks wisely.

2100 hours

Desperately wishing I was anywhere but here, Gurli and I

creep through the gloomy rat-swamped tunnels under the King's Castle. Thankfully, the oil lamps in our ivory-knuckled paws do a good job of keeping the shadows at bay, but I still feel pins of terror prickling my scalp. I'm claustrophobic, the sickeningly low roof and the mouldy walls a tomb to me.

'These tunnels were mostly dug in the beginning of the 1700s,' Gurli whispers. 'Mostly. King Carl XI was on the Swedish throne back then but he was often away fighting, expanding his empire...'

Her soft springy words and the pad of her feet soothe me, helping to keep my mind off the tons of dirt piled up just a foot or so over the tops of our skulls.

Only a half hour ago, Gurli's father had flapped his hand at the pantry, and there, in the corner, I had discovered his daughter scraping the skin of filthy carrots.

I had asked her, blankly, if there is a tunnel under Vita havet.

'Yes, there is,' she had told me, dropping the carrots, a playful spark in her eye. 'But there's no way you will find it on your own. I had better show you.' Then she had grinned and her eyes had lit up like a child just let out of school.

I had rolled my eyes, tutted, and in my best schoolmaster's

tone, I had told the plucky lass to loose the anklets of silver bells. Then she had led me to a hidden door in the back of the pantry.

Now, seemingly lost in this maze of tiny tunnels, I keep tight on her heels, happy she is here. I just hope she will not be hurt. I'm very fond of Gurli. She's clever, funny too and full of tomorrows. The thought of losing my sister and her....

'...so now, if the castle is ever attacked, the king and his family can escape through the tunnels to a ship.'

'Clever,' I murmur.

Suddenly, a rat scampers over my boot. I swallow and a cold chill floods my body; perhaps I'm allergic to cat-sized rats too.

'In 1759, King Adolf Fredrik and his queen, Lovisa Ulrika of Prussia, were the first royals to enjoy the luxury of the new palace...'

'How is it you know so much history?' I interrupt her.

'I creep in Bernadotte Library every night to read,' she explains. 'I want to be an inventor, you see. Alfred Nobel, he's the best inventor in the world and he's Swedish...'

'I just met him,' I say nonchalantly.

She stops so suddenly, I almost knock her over. 'Alfred Nobel!?'

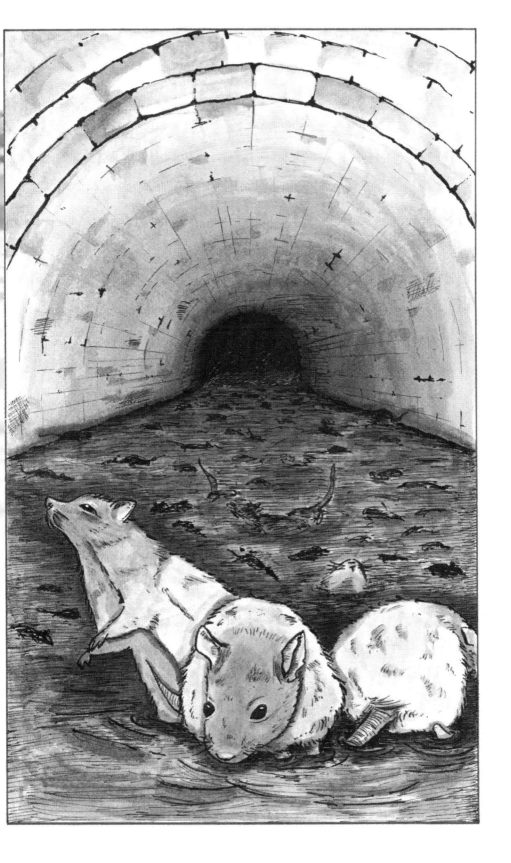

I nod. 'At the king's party.'

'No! NO WAY!'

'Honestly.'

The look of astonishment in her eyes pulls a smile from my lips.

'After we stop Duchess Solbakken, we will try to find him and you can meet him too,' I promise her.

'Wow! Thank you.' She hugs me tightly. 'Did you know,' she whispers to the folds of my tunic, 'he just discovered a way of blowing up nitro-glycerine. He thinks, when he shows everybody how powerful it is, nobody will risk a war...'

I scowl. Alfred Nobel's a fool; but that's not why I'm scowling. Just in front of us there is a soft glow. Gently, I grip Gurli's shoulders and step away, putting my finger to her lips. The history lesson instantly stops.

'Keep in the shadows,' I murmur. 'Try not to let her see you.'

She nods.

With my knees knocking up a drum roll and with my sword in my hand, I creep around the corner, and the next, and the next and there I discover a mammoth cavern lit up by lanterns. It looks to be almost identical in size to Vita havet and I feel instantly better.

But I do not feel better for long.

I spot a number of pillars holding up the roof and in the very middle of the room, looking unnervingly smug, stands Duchess Solbakken.

'Hello there, Major,' she booms, her words bouncing off the cavern walls. 'I was beginning to get chilly. What took you so long?'

With a dry mouth, I trudge slowly over to her, stopping three feet short of her protruding belly. She is holding a candle and the tip of a long, winding fuse, and I quickly see why. Each of the pillars has a barrel roped snugly to it.

'Gunpowder,' she tells me matter-of-factly. 'Three tons of it. In a second or two, perhaps three, the fuse will be lit and twenty-two seconds later, perhaps twenty-three,' she's playing with me now, 'KABOOM! The pillars will blow up, the roof will collapse in and it will be drizzling royalty.'

I think I can see all the barrels of gunpowder. I count twelve; too many to get to in only twenty or so seconds. The only thing I can do is keep my wits, keep her talking and hope Gurli's bully of a father tells Gripenstedt and the troops hunting for me where I went.

'Duchess…'

She tuts. 'I'm no Duchess, My Sweet,' she chirrups,

dropping her posh Oslo accent and replacing it with London cockney. 'She's keeping her family company in a very damp cellar in Norway.'

'You were impersonating Duchess Solbakken.' I murmur. Then a bolt of lightning hits me. Every member of the family had had different coloured eyes. 'All four of you were impostors,' I wheeze. No wonder Astrid had not remembered she had a pet hamster called Elephant. She had not been Astrid Solbakken.

'Yes, Major, the duke and his family had never even been to Stockholm so nobody in the royal court has ever met them. Perfect. We duped the lot of 'em.'

'And there had been no servants at the Solbakken's villa,' I recall.

'Nah, we threw 'em in the cellar too. Too risky to let 'em go. They'd only run off to the town copper.' She sniggers, her eyes dancing in sickly glee. 'They must be cooking the chef by now, or the butler and his kids.'

'But I met the butler,' I blurt out, recalling his sharp eyes and bulldog jaw.

The assassin's lips tip up. There is a secret there and I wonder what it is.

'Then the prince of Denmark's puppy-dog shows up.' She

eyes me scornfully. 'You, Major Tor. But we knew General de Wimpffen planned to send you to Copenhagen to pay off his poker debt to Frederick. And we knew Frederick then planned to send you to stop us.'

'But how?'

'Your royal boss had a spy in our London HQ. But we captured him and we er, helped him to remember what the Danish prince was up to.'

The eyeballs in the box of toffees!

Almost absentmindedly, I kick a rat off my boot; her story still did not add up. 'You knew my orders were to stop you, but yet you did not murder me when the highwayman knocked me out.'

She shrugs. 'SWARM's orders were to kill you,' she admits. 'We even attempted to…'

'The Japanese cook on the Flying Spur,' I butt in angrily.

'Yes, Mr Grasshopper. His brother, Mr Wasp, is going to be awfully upset and, trust me, he's not the sort of chap you want to upset.' She smirks evilly. 'Anyway, SWARM eventually decided to let you tag along. A trooper sent by the prince of Denmark to protect us from highwaymen, even if you were only pretending, would add credibility to our story.

'There was a bonus too,' she adds. 'With King Karl in his

tomb and the Solbakken family being accused of his murder, you'd be there, Major, to stoke the fire; to tell the weeping citizens of Sweden how much the Solbakkens of Norway despised the Swedish. That's why we helped you to find a room in the castle; to keep you here.'

I feel as if a blindfold has been ripped from my eyes. 'And that's why the boy, Bertil, or whatever the impostor's name was, did his little performance in the wagon, pretending to loathe the Swedish and Karl XV. Just for me.' I flex my jaw. I had been just a tool to them; a balloon in SWARM's breeze.

Cocking her thumb, the assassin shoots me with her index finger. 'Exactly. The Solbakkens will be blamed and a very angry Sweden will declare war on Norway.'

'How very tidy,' I ridicule her. 'Then Norway will run to Denmark for help.'

She laughs scornfully; a sort of trillish 'opera singer' snigger. 'The idiot paying SWARM thinks Sweden will be too scared to attack both Norway and Denmark. Fool! There'll be war and SWARM will be very busy working for, well, everybody. It'll be payday every day.'

My mouth drops open, the scope of the assassins' plan sinking in. 'But why murder every person in the room?' I quiz her. 'Even the queen?'

Her eyebrows knot; her pupils shift up and left. I don't think she knows.

'Oops!' I mock her. 'Did your boss - Mr Spider, is it - not tell you why? Did he not trust you?'

A look of hurt and bewilderment shadows her eyes. Then she seems to recover and blurts out, 'I s'ppose the lad did not gallop off back to Oslo. We assumed he had deserted; decided the job was too risky and scarpered.'

'No.' I jump at the opportunity to fire a second shot. 'He is at the bottom of a very deep well just by the Wily Wolf Inn.'

But my petty attempt is lost on the cold assassin. 'Good for you, Major. Annoying boy. Anyway, he's got company; we tossed the three highwaymen in there too.'

I inwardly cringe, remembering the dull thud when I had dropped the killer in the well.

'We had to, you see. Too risky to hand them over to a nosey copper.' Her brow furrows. 'I s'ppose you also murdered my other two co-conspirators.'

'I shot your sniper, yes, but the duke, or whoever he was, killed himself.'

'Excellent! The old fellow was just hired help. The boy too. Poor minstrels in need of work. Now SWARM need not pay them.' She puffs up her cheeks. 'But Astrid, Miss

Butterfly we call her, well, Mr Spider will not be a happy fellow. To put it mildly.'

I eye her, scowling. 'I thought Duke Solbakken must be Locust, but he's not, Locust is you.'

'Oh no, My Sweet,' she chirrups with a condescending snigger. 'They call me Granny Moth.'

'Then who is…?'

But with the flamboyance of a circus clown, she taps the tip of the fuse to the wick of the candle and, instantly, there is a burst of sparks. A split second later, every fuse in the cavern is lit, and I watch, hypnotised, the red and yellow embers race over to the deadly barrels of powder.

I look up to see where the assassin is, but all I spot is the hem of her dress flapping down a tunnel.

With a mop of my clammy brow, I hurry over to the closest fuse and with the heel of my boot, I crush the dancing sparks. Then the next and the next…

Gurli sprints from the shadows to copy me and my spirits lift. The cocky assassin had not reckoned on there being two of us. Maybe we can do this.

Maybe…

I run over to a barrel, my heel smothering yet another ember.

STAMP! STAMP! STAMP!

'That's it, Tor,' Gurli yells jubilantly.

I stop, my lungs in agony, but there is still a menacing hiss in the cavern. With terror flooding my body and trying to unlock my knees, I look over to a shadowy corner of the cave. There! I spy a thirteenth pillar, and hugging it, a thirteenth barrel of gunpowder, the spitting tip of a fuse only a foot away.

'RUN!' I cry, grabbing for Gurli's hand. We sprint for the tunnel the assassin had escaped down.

BOOM! A crash of thunder ricochets off the cavern walls.

I hit the floor, rocks tumbling over me, cutting and slicing, scraping my skin and smashing my knee. In agony, I pull Gurli free of the rubble and cradle her in my arms.

'Gurli!' I cry. 'GURLI!' But she has no last words for me. The spark has already vanished from her eyes.

I look back up the tunnel to the cavern. My lantern's still lit and I see the roof is still up. Only the pillar has been destroyed. The king and his subjects will see the sunrise after all. Then, reluctantly, my eyes rest on the face of Gurli. It is as if a star has blinked out from my sky. My frozen soul will not let me weep; all I can do is shut my eyes and press her cheek to my chest.

I will miss her smile.

'Forever young,' I murmur.

I clamber to my feet, a terrible, all-consuming lust for revenge gripping my soul. I draw my sword but I see the tip is snapped off. No matter. I pick up the lantern and limp up the tunnel. I can still stab the harlot with the blunt end.

In fact, it will hurt more.

Turning a corner, the tunnel abruptly stops. I see I'm just by the docks and with the help of the lazy moon I spy Moth climbing into a rowing boat.

Incensed, I toss my lantern after her. 'Your plan did not work,' I cry. 'Most of your bombs did not blow up. The roof did not fall.'

She glowers back at me, her hawkish eyes icy cold, her cheeks turning an ugly patchy violet. 'Watch your back, Major,' she jeers.

NO!' I cry, inflamed, my blood disobeying the cold wind and bubbling in my ears. 'YOU WATCH YOURS!'

Powerless, I watch my enemy drift off over the river, stopping by the beefy hull of a silvery iron ship. A rocket from the birthday party zooms up in the sky and blows up in a shower of red and yellow stars and for a split second I see the words 'Goyo-Goyuku' emblazoned on the bow. The ship I had seen from Gripenstedt's balcony. But my mind is too numb to worry and it hardly sinks in.

I drop to my knees, a broken sword in my hand and a broken spirit in my chest, left to wallow in my very own river of hurt.

I sit there for, I don't know, forever maybe, till the words, 'Good evening, Major,' pull me from my stupor.

Rallying the last of my strength, I look up. The rowing boat has returned from the ship and climbing out of it is a man in a German cavalry uniform.

'Colonel Von der Tann,' I silently mouth, my eyes the size of barrel tops.

Whistling a cheery tune, he strolls over to me. He plonks his feet so firmly on the floor I doubt even a herd of elephants would uproot him.

'Yes,' he claps his hands, rubbing the palms, 'and no. You see, I'm also your mysterious Locust and a member of SWARM, the Sepulchre of World Assassins, Ransomers and Mutineers.' He chews on his thumb perhaps to allow me time for the news to sink in. 'I must say, Major Tor, you did a wonderful job destroying my plan. I'm awfully upset with you.'

'Too bad,' I retort gruffly, still on my knees.

So Von der Tann works for SWARM too. No wonder he had known where to find me on the docks in France. The prince of Denmark's spy in London had probably told SWARM under torture of Frederick's plan and SWARM had told him.

'In France you told me you never kill in cold blood,' I say frostily. 'Pretty difficult for any assassin to pull off.'

'Yes. Yes, it is,' he says cheerily. 'Well, I see your blade there is broken. Anyway, you look way too hurt to be duelling with swords, so pistols it is.' I spy two muskets hooked on his fancy silver belt; he hands me the smallest. 'Probably for the best. You did not fight very gentlemanly in France. A swordfight is for swords, not boots, elbows and er, coffee beans. Up you get then, Trooper. Time to pay the piper.'

I clamber drunkenly to my feet and stonily eyeball the German, but I see two, no, three of him; my eyes will not focus. Probably from the blow to my skull from the falling rocks.

'Just the three steps, I think,' Von der Tann chirrups up. 'It is awfully cramped in this tunnel and your knee looks a little bloody.'

Jadedly, I nod, cocking the pistol.

'Why, Colonel?' I croak. 'Why did you do all of this?'

Von der Tann titters, a mocking twinkle in his eye. 'Not for Germany, not for God, not even for the lady I love and, trust me, I do love her. A jewel, Old Chap. A ruby in a tiny silver chest.'

My lips curls up in a snarl and my eyes sharpen.

We stand back to back.

'One.'

SWARM had murdered my poor Gurli for a shiny rock in a box.

'Two.'

She had just been a pawn; a casualty of war.

'THREE!'

Forever young!

With red fury exploding in my chest, I twist on my heel and…

BOOM!

2316 hours, Stockholm Docks

The Goyo-Goyuko is not a pretty ship, her grey deck a hotchpotch of rusty bolts and bubbly welds. Her hull is pitted with cannon ports and two funnels burst up from her bowls,

the tops sharp-toothed and splayed.

Hidden in the shadow of the port funnel, Granny Moth eyeballs the two dimly-lit forms on the wharf. It seems Major Tor had told her a porky; he did not murder Butterfly after all. But who, the elderly assassin wonders, is she talking to. A man by the look of the sword on his hip. A secret lover, perhaps. Moth scowls. Well, she is annoyingly pretty. But it is too misty to see the man properly and, anyway, the solitary lantern on the Goyo-Goyuko's deck is no match for a moonless sky.

She sees Butterfly turn on her heels and march over to the ship. 'I trust he's worth it,' the man calls to her. Then, he too strolls away.

Granny Moth stays in the shadows till Butterfly drops to the Goyo-Goyuko's iron deck. Then, swiftly, she steps over to her. 'AHOY THERE!' she hollers. 'Major Tor told me he shot you.'

Butterfly jumps, dropping the bag of golf clubs she is carrying on her foot and almost toppling off the deck. Seeing who it is, her eyes narrow. 'Thankfully, Major Tor can't hit a sleeping elephant in a zoo,' she says curtly. 'The bullet just grazed my ribs.'

'Oh! My poor sweety. Let me see.' Moth's stumpy fingers

fly to the young assassin's shoulder strap but a cold hand slaps them away.

'Never forget who I am,' she tells her frostily.

'Yes, yes. Sorry,' blusters Moth, stepping hastily back. 'Just er, trying to help.'

'Help! HELP! Your only job was to blow up the castle. Tell me, and be honest now, how difficult is it to put a match to a fuse?'

Crossly, Moth puckers up her lips. 'I followed Mr Locust's orders to the letter; to the full stop in fact. He told me to rope the barrels to the...' She stops and rubs her whiskery chin. 'Why is it, My Lady,' she says slowly, 'we attempted to blow up everybody at the party and not just the King?'

Butterfly eyes her thoughtfully. 'Why do you want to know?'

'Oh, well er, it just cropped up. Mr Locust actually, yesterday, in the tunnel; he asked me and I, well...'

'Mr Locust, you say.' The young assassin frowns. 'How odd. I thought he knew. I wonder, did it not perhaps just 'crop up' with Major Tor?'

'No, no, I er...'

'As you well know, Mr Spider enjoys his secrets. If he deemed it unnecessary to tell you then I strongly recommend

you do not ask.'

'Mr Spider tells me everything,' retorts Moth huffily.

'Really,' murmurs Butterfly with a cynical arch of her eyebrows.

Annoyed, the elderly assassin blurts out, 'Tor murdered Mr Locust. He shot him in the chest in the tunnel.'

Wide-eyed, Butterfly sucks in her cheeks. 'His Lordship will not be happy,' she mutters.

Moth swallows and a whimper slips her lips. She drops her eyes to her stiletto boots. 'The er, fellow on the dock just now,' she begins tentatively, 'he…'

'Is not your concern.' She eyes her expectantly and Moth hastily nods.

Pulling off her shawl, the elderly assassin slips it over Butterfly's shoulders. 'Only a dress in September!' she scolds her. 'You must be terribly cold.'

Butterfly surrenders and allows her to knot the woolly tips. 'You worry too much,' she relents, elbowing Moth softly in the ribs. 'Now, to work. Where's the prisoner?'

'Below deck, My Lady. Cuffed, gagged and not very happy.'

Good! Tell the skipper to pull up anchor. We must be in London by Wednesday; there's a very important job to do in

Oxford so tell him not to dilly dally. I want Goyo-Goyuku's top speed.'

She picks up the set of clubs and hands them to Moth. 'In the pockets you will find the golf balls with the powder and shot hidden in them.'

The old assassin nods and bobs off a curtsy. 'Is the musket in here too?'

'No, it dropped off the clock tower when I was shot.' Butterfly rubs her brow and her shoulders droop dejectedly. 'I thought Mr Locust's plan was foolproof. We planned for months: the Oslo accents, every nut and bolt of the Solbakken's family tree jammed up here,' she jabs her temple sharply with her thumb, 'but in the end it all went belly up.'

A tiny sneer widens Moth's nostrils. 'Major Tor is a cancer,' she rasps, adding her twopennyworth.

'Yes.' Butterfly nods thoughtfully, her eyes hooded and sorrowful. 'He did put a spanner in the works.' She looks to the other SWARM assassin. 'You did well, by the way, snatching Mr Locust's body from the tunnel.'

Moth's eyebrows arch hawkishly. 'How did you know...?'

'Is not important.' She plays idly with the knot on the scarf. 'Did you er, see the major there? Was he badly injured?'

'Oh yes, I spotted the meddling idiot. He had a few cuts, a bloody knee...'

'He's no idiot,' Butterfly interrupts her. 'He stopped SWARM.'

Moth's plump shoulders pop up indifferently. 'Anyway, he was out cold in the rubble but a king's trooper showed up so I had no time to, you know...' To illustrate, she cocks her thumb and shoots the ship's port funnel with her index finger.

Butterfly nods understandingly. 'Don't worry, Major Tor will soon perish. No doubt Mr Spider will see to it personally.'

Eyes shadowed, the young assassin chomps on her bottom lip. 'We will drop Mr Locust's body in the English Channel. He can help Mr Grasshopper to feed the fish.'

Moth pulls a pink hanky from her pocket, puts it to her lips and titters.

'Not a joke,' snaps Butterfly.

'Oh! Sorry.' She chews on the hanky's lacy corner. 'Do you think Mr Spider will be terribly upset that we er, botched the job?'

Butterfly looks to her, a hint of sympathy in her pencil-thin lips. She puts her hand on Moth's shoulder. 'It is not in his character to show mercy,' she tells her soberly.

'But - but the plan was Mr - Mr Locust's,' she protests, jitters distorting her words. 'We must put the blunder on his doorstep.' Her eyes narrow evilly. 'Or on the doorstep of the Danish prince, Frederick; he sent Major Tor to stop us.'

'No,' snaps Butterfly. 'I will shoulder the responsibility.' She swallows and musters a jaded smile. 'His Lordship will not hurt his only pup.'

Twirling on her heels, she slips down a set of iron steps to a corridor. It is carpeted blood-red, hundreds of stuffed blowfish, reef sharks and gigantic turtle shells hooked to the walls. She strolls over to her cabin door, the fifth on the left, and, softly, she slips in.

For a second or two, she rests her brow on the cold door. Then, with a trembling hand, she bolts it shut. Slowly, like a murderess on her way to the hangman's noose, she tows her feet over to the mirror by her four-poster bed. There, she pulls off the shawl and unhooks the strap of her dress.

Her skin is deathly pale accentuating the blackened hole in her chest. Almost reverently, she puts her finger to it, gently tracing the scorched rim. It looks to be the size of a copper penny, instantly fatal to anybody but her...

...and her monstrosity of a father.

'Bullseye, Major Tor,' she mutters.

Monday, 21st September, 1870

504 Days to Assassination Day

1350 hours, Aytré, South of France

Wednesday, 2nd September, 1870

Hello my darling mother,

I hope this letter finds you in good spirits and Renee is following my strict orders, to stop you working every hour of every day and to sleep in on Sundays.

I'm presently camped in La Moncelle, a tiny town in Northern France, under the command of General de Wimpffen. Every day, our cannons and bayonets put pay to many a German's devilish plans for our beloved land. But the news, I'm sorry to say, is still not good.

Our army is terribly outnumbered and William R

182

Gladstone, the British prime minister, who we thought was our ally, has chosen not to send us the troops we so desperately need. It is a terrible blow and General de Wimpffen is very upset. It will, I fear, result in France soon falling to her enemy. Our country is indeed misfortunate to be neighbours with the blood-thirsty Germans and the cowardly English.

Soon General de Wimpffen will order us to attack the enemy stronghold of Floing. I fear it is a fool's errand and, I must tell you, I do not expect to live. I know this will hurt you terribly but it is important you stay strong. A terrible storm is on the horizon and the Fiquet Winery will need you by the helm. You must try to find safe harbour for the company father loved so much.

I will entrust this letter to a fellow cavalryman, a Major Tor. He is Swedish and a mercenary but I find him to be honest and trustworthy. I am confident he will cross shark-infested waters to see it is posted to you.

A bird is singing in the tree by my tent. A robin, I think. Morning, it seems, is with us. So soon, but still I welcome it.

I will always be your loving son,

Ludovic

Cupping her wet cheeks in her hands, Scarlet Fiquet drops jadedly to the velvet sofa in her late-husband's study.

Ludovic, her only son, lost. And she had not been there to comfort him. She is tormented. In her mind's eye she sees him sprawled in a pool of blood, her little boy who loved to play chess. He weeps for his mother but she is not there. Nobody is. Nobody to hold his hand and to help him to say his prayers.

'Our Father, who art in heaven, hallowed be thy name...'

There is the softest of knocks on the door.

With a monumental effort, Scarlet sits up, struggling to pry off the coppery curls plastered to her wet cheeks. 'It's er, open,' she says, her words husky and peppered with splinters. She's in no mood for hollow sympathy and sorrowful eyes but she cannot cower in the study forever.

Scarlet's doddery old butler, Renee, totters in, his knees badly in need of a squirt of oil, the heels of his carpet slippers scuffing the cherrywood floor. 'Sorry to disturb you, Madam, but, well,' his shoulders pop up apologetically and he hands her a newspaper, 'bad news from Paris.'

It is, it seems, a week for bad news.

With a jittery serpent twisting in her stomach, she unfolds it and looks in horror on the words,

GERMANS OVERRUN PARIS
FRANCE SURRENDERS

Wildly, Scarlet looks to her butler but there is no shoulder to cry on there. There is only terror in the old man's eyes and the frantic need for her, for anybody, to tell him what to do. Hastily, she masks her own terror. She must be strong for the loyal men and women who work for the Fiquet Winery. This, she knows, is just the beginning. The Germans will not stop in Paris.

'Who knows of this?' she snaps.

'Just you and me, Madame. Oh, and Albert, the paperboy, but he'll be over in Aytré by now.'

She nods thoughtfully. 'I must meet with the staff.' Struggling to her feet, she begins to pace the study. Here is a job she can put her mind to. Better to fill her days with work than with thoughts of her poor Ludovic glassy-eyed in a ditch. 'Say in two hours in the library,' she tells him. 'Go to the scullery and ask Édith to put on coffee and bake cherry buns.' She recalls what her husband, Philippe, had always told her. Bad news with good food is easy to swallow.

'Yes, Madame.' The butler's chin lifts and a hook pulls on the corner of his lips. He seems happy now; now he too has a job to do.

Creaking like an old rocking chair, he teeters off. But then, just by the door, he stops. 'I'm so terribly sorry for you loss,' he murmurs. 'I remember when Ludovic was just a boy playing chess with his father.'

Scarlet knows this must be difficult for Renee. He's old school and not given to displays of sentimentally.

'You know, I think, perhaps, he let the boy win…'

'He did,' she cuts him off. The memory hurts too much to linger on.

She steps up to him and puts her hand softly on his bony shoulder. His skin, she sees, is thin and papery and he looks lost in his butler's uniform.

'I will miss him,' the old man says simply.

'I know.' She swallows. 'So will I. But we will remember him.'

'Yes.' He nods determinedly. 'Yes, Madame, we will.' And with a poignant smile, he totters from the room.

Scarlet, left for a moment with her own turbulent thoughts, wanders over to the bay windows. From up here on the hill she can see almost every foot of the valley and the sprawling vineyards of Chateau Fiquet. The half a century old winery had been left to her by her husband, a truly wonderful man who had not deserved the agony of bowl cancer. The hidden enemy nobody can fight.

Soon, she knows, the Germans will march south to the city of Bordeaux and the Spanish border. They will probably march on Aytré too. Then what? Will they commandeer her villa? Put a match to the winery?

She balls up her hand, crumpling up the letter. In her torment, she had forgotten she had it. Hastily, she flattens it out on her knee and there, in the words of her son, she finds a target for her spent up fury.

'William R Gladstone.' Tasting the words, they feel bitter on her tongue. Plums picked in May.

The man's a coward, the blood of hundreds of Frenchmen on his hands. The blood of her poor son on his hands.

But here is an enemy she can see, who she can hurt.

He will pay for what he did.

She turns to the room, her gaze brushing a grandfather clock and a faded watercolour of a tree by a pond and a herd of gloomy-eyed cows. Her eyes stop to linger on the cabinet by the door and a rather cobwebby bottle of wine trying unsuccessfully to hide there.

The legendary 1787 Lafite and probably the only bottle left in the world.

Squaring her shoulders, she storms over to it and plucks it to her chest.

She remembers her husband had always kept a corkscrew in the bottom drawer of the cabinet, a 50th birthday present from Ludovic, the bishop-shaped handle perfectly sculpted in African ivory. She drops to her knees and pulls the drawer open and there she finds it, nestled intimately by a slightly dog-eared copy of the bible. For a moment, her hand hovers over the book; but no, she will not find any answers in there.

Grabbing up the corkscrew, the uncorks the bottle with

188

expert hands. 'To the British prime minister.' She toasts the clock's swinging pendulum. 'May the murderer rot in hell.' Then she puts it to her lips and drinks.

Now she must find a way to put him there.

Friday, 25th September, 1870
501 Days to Assassination Day

1350 hours, Stockholm Hospital

Today is my birthday; I am twenty-six years old but I feel a lot, lot older.

I lay silently on my bed, my glassy eyes to the open window and the unhappy stoop of a willow tree swaying in the breeze. It is six days later and my knee is still a swollen mess, my body a jumbled map of cuts and purpling bumps. Even the scar on my cheek is still all gummy and red. But, for all my discomfort, my only thought is of Gurli.

She had had such a terrible life, lost her mum to dysentery, her dad a bully. I remember how skinny she had been and the swollen bump over her eye. She had just been a tiny flower; a

189

tiny flower in a forest of weeds.

A raw throbbing ache floods me, but I embrace it, cementing it to my armour, to my walls, to hold in the hurt till I can exact my revenge on SWARM and the assassin, Granny Moth.

They will pay for what they did to her.

The door to my room opens with a pop, rudely awakening me from my vengeful thoughts. I look up expecting to see my Swedish sentry or the scowl of the gigantic-bosomed matron; I do not expect to see the hooded silhouette of Prince Frederick of Denmark,

'Major Tor,' he greets me, eyeing my scabby knee and screwing up his nose. 'Been in the wars, I see.'

'My Prince!' I sit up, my chin hitting my collar bone in a sort of bow. 'Sorry I cannot get up…'

'No, no, Old Fellow, you need your rest.' His murky eyes narrow and for a second I think he still expects me to hop off my bed and drop to my pulped knee.

Slipping off his hood, he pulls up a stool, drops a silk hanky on it, and sits. I spy the sword, Tyrfing, on his hip and I wet my lips.

'So, Major, I suppose the food in here is awful.'

But the throb of my cheek and knee put me in no mood for

chitchat, even with a crown prince. 'How can I be of help, Sire?' I ask him bluntly, my neck quickly rediscovering the comfy hollow in the pillow.

He eyes me coldly. 'In truth, I'm in Stockholm to help you. I stayed on after Karl's birthday to do a spot of hunting with him. Deer mostly - and rabbits.'

I scowl; oddly, I do not recollect seeing him at the party.

'That's my story, anyway. I'm actually here to tidy up the mess you left.'

I chew on my bottom lip, my gaze even colder than his.

'So, Major,' he narrows his eyes, wrinkling up his crows feet, 'let's begin by you telling me everything.' He rests his chin on his fist. 'EVERYTHING!'

Inhaling deeply, I do exactly that.

I tell him how the four SWARM assassins had impersonated the Solbakken family, how his spy in London had told SWARM under torture of my mission and how my old enemy, Colonel Von der Tann of the Seventh German Cavalry who I had shot in the chest, and not a member of the Oslo family, had been the infamous Locust.

The prince rubs his chin thoughtfully. 'So many assassins for only six hundred kronor,' he whispers almost to himself.

But I catch his words and a scowl knots my eyebrows, my

thoughts racing. Almost absentmindedly, I fiddle with the rabbit's foot in my wet salty paw.

'The Swedish king must know by now of the attempt on his life,' I say forlornly, 'and that the assassins' paymaster was Norway.'

The memory of poor Gurli and what she did will now be trampled on by a bloody war.

'Lord, no!' Frederick smirks. 'Karl's a fool. He thinks Duke Solbakken just keeled over; too many cups of punch. Oh, and the body by the clock tower has been er, dumped in the river.'

Astrid! It hurts but I try not to show it. I had liked her and now I will never even know who she was. Poetry written in water.

'By...?'

'My spy. A different spy.' His lips curl humourlessly. 'He still has his eyeballs.'

Suddenly, I remember the Solbakkens and I try to sit up, my knee yelping in protest. 'The family in Oslo and the servants, they must still be in the cellar.'

'Calm yourself, Major.' He pats my shoulder, his fingers icy cold. 'When I arrived for the party, albeit three hours delayed by a jammed rudder...'

So that's why I had not spotted him there.

'...I was shown the body of the duke and I knew instantly it was not him. We play poker, you see. So I sent two of my best troopers to Oslo to rescue the Solbakken family. They just sent word; the family is fit and well, the chef and the butler too, and, er, a little merry. It seems the cellar they were imprisoned in was very well stocked with wine. Just wine.' He smirks. 'Probably not so well stocked now.'

Despite this good news, the prince is annoying me. He is so maddeningly pompous. I think he thinks I'm just a toddler and he's explaining how two plus two equals four.

'Oh,' I put on a show of just remembering, 'the assassin pretending to be the son; I dropped him in a well just by the Wily Wolf Inn in Karlstad.'

The prince's perfectly trimmed eyebrows climb his brow. 'A well, you say. Major, how very inventive of you.'

'I think you will discover three highwaymen in there too,' I add, enjoying the look of astonishment in his potlid eyes. I can tell he is not relishing being the last man to know. 'Murdered, but not by my hand.'

He nods stiffly. 'My men will see to it.'

'So the only assassin left on my 'TO KILL' list is Granny Moth,' I snarl.

The prince furrows his brow.

'She's the old bat who pretended to be Duchess Solbakken and attempted to blow up the castle. She escaped on a ship called the Goyo-Goyuku.'

'I see. Pity.' The words scalpel sharp. 'A sentry did however discover the body of a girl in the rubble.' Gurli! My guts twist in agony. 'Her father, I think he's a chef in the castle, he plans to bury her tomorrow. Naturally, he's very upset.'

'I bet he is,' I murmur with a snort. 'Now he has nobody to bully.'

My cheeks feel hot, my lips horribly dry. I bend my knee experimentally. It still hurts, but not with the deep life-sapping throb of six days ago. Anyway, it is of no matter; I will attend the funeral even if I must hobble there.

'But there was no sign of any German cavalry officer,' Frederick tells me. 'Perhaps this Moth-woman took the body.'

'Hmm. Perhaps.' My thoughts still on Gurli. 'How did the king's trooper find me?' I ask him dully.

'I was told, when you thumped Lord Gripenstedt he yelled for a sentry. The sentry went after you, and this girl's father told him you had kidnapped his daughter and took her to the tunnels. He discovered you out cold on the…'

'KIDNAPPED!' I cry, Frederick's words finally penetrating my numb mind. I look to him wide-eyed. 'And I suppose that is why there is now a sentry on the door to my room.'

The prince nods. 'That, and the fact you murdered Lord Gripenstedt's son.' He shoots me a stony look. 'How very barbaric of you, Major.'

'Gripenstedt's son murdered my sister,' I retort hotly.

'Did he now?' The corner of his lip curls up. 'I see.'

But I know he can't. To him, the blood of Sylva is no trade for the noble blood of a lord's son.

'Anyway,' says the prince, carrying on, 'I bribed the sentry who discovered you not to tell anybody he also discovered a number of bombs in the tunnel. It seems they were not so far from where you had fallen.'

The rest of the barrels roped to the pillars! Thankfully, they had not blown up too.

Frederick scowls. 'I wonder how SWARM transported them there.'

I look to him blankly but I think I know how. Yesterday, when I had been under Gripenstedt's balcony, I had seen Granny Moth on her balcony with the lantern. I bet she had been signalling to the Goyo-Goyuku; letting Locust know it

was safe to carry the barrels up the secret tunnel from the docks to the cavern under Vita havet.

But I do not tell Frederick this. Why not? Well, to be honest, and I know this is a little childish, but it just dawned on me that the Crown Prince of Denmark, for all his pomp and worldly ways, is a total and utter stinker.

We sit in silence for a moment, then, 'My Lord, how did you know the assassins cost six hundred kronor?'

The prince smirks. 'Simple, Norway is not SWARM's paymaster, I am.'

'YOU!?' I was correct; he IS a stinker.

He rests his elbows on his knees, steepling his fingers under his chin. 'I thought if the Swedish king was assassinated and Norway blamed, Sweden would threaten to attack them. Norway would then look to Denmark to protect them and my father would double his lands overnight. Lands I will inherit when I'm crowned king.'

'But you got cold feet.'

'Yes,' he nods, 'Sweden is too powerful. My military adviser, General de Meza, told me, a little belatedly, even with Denmark's support the Swedish would still attack, and win, and I would end up the ruler of nowhere. With Norway and my country overrun, Karl would probably pack me, my father and the rest of my family off to Scotland and I would spend the rest of my days living off sheep's stomach.

'I did attempt to cancel the hit; I even offered SWARM a second chest full of jewels...'

'War's good for profits,' I butt in bitterly. 'Payday every day,' I murmur, echoing Granny Moth's chilling prophecy. 'SWARM probably jammed your ship's rudder too. You knew Duke Solbakken. They did not want you to see his imposter at the party and blow the plan.'

He looks to me fleetingly, his dark eyes critical of my words. Then he nods his understanding. 'I had to find a way to stop SWARM. Sadly, Locust's boss, Mr Spider, insisted I pay him upfront for the hit; a ruby, six hundred kronor's worth in a tiny silver chest, so I called in a debt and de Wimpffen sent me you.'

Gritting my teeth, I watch him tip up the stool and walk over to the door. The sheer cheek of the man. 'Major, you did a wonderful job; you stopped a lot of unnecessary bloodshed. I applaud you.'

'You sly son of a...'

'Now, now, Trooper,' his eyes burn the back of my pupils, 'remember your manners.'

'So if you think I did such a wonderful job hand over my

reward: the sword and the hundred kronor.'

'Major, Major,' he mocks me. 'To what end? The Swedish plan to execute you for the murder of Lord Gripenstedt's son and the kidnapping of the chef's child.' His lips twist and in his cold eyes I see a vulture. 'The only reward for you, I'm sorry to say, will be a pauper's coffin in a very shallow hole.'

Popping up his hood, he clicks his heels. 'Good day.'

He strolls over to the door, but there, he stops. 'By the way, Alfred Nobel was kidnapped from the party. Nobody knows who by. I don't suppose...'

I snort. He still expects me to help him.

'No matter. Undoubtedly a ransom demand will follow shortly; then we will know.'

In horror I watch the door slam shut. He says a few words to my sentry, but, muffled by the door, I do not catch them. Orders to shoot me, no doubt, if I try to run off.

So I had just been a pawn in SWARM's and the Danish prince's deadly game. A twig in a raging river.

In fury, I toss the rabbit's foot out of the window. I will no longer put my trust in luck or in the corrupt hands of de Wimpffen or Frederick, so-called 'privileged men'. Now, I will only trust the tip of my sword and the bullet in the barrel of my musket.

One Year Later

Monday, 25th September, 1871

136 Days to Assassination Day

2245 hours, Copenhagen, Denmark

Today is my birthday; I am twenty-seven years old but I feel a lot, lot older.

Keeping a firm hold on the rope, I toss the hook over the wall. I pull it and it anchors. Then, hand over hand, foot over foot, I scramble up. Once on the top, I quickly pull up the rope, re-anchor it and drop to the freshly cut lawn.

On tiptoe, I creep through the trees. I spy the ghostly shadow of a sentry, no, two of them. Luckily, they're too busy discussing the Hviids, a new tavern in the town, and they do not spot me. Keeping perfectly still till they pass me by, I then sprint from the safety of the trees and over to the north wall of Denmark's Royal Palace.

I kneel by a window. Using a hanky to mask the splintering glass, I smash it with a rock. Simple, but effective.

I stay absolutely still and try not to pant. Too many hours spent in London pubs and now I'm awfully unfit. The cut on my cheek is throbbing too. Even now, a full year on, it hurts.

But there's no running feet, no yells for, 'HELP!' Just the chitter of insects and the fluted whistle of a hungry bullfinch.

I hop up on the sill, lift my knees to my chin and twist. My shoulder bumps the wood, my sword too, but a second later I drop unhurt to the scullery floor.

Confidently, I set off for Prince Frederick's bedchamber. It took me over a month to plan this little escapade, so I know the route. I run up twenty steps, counting them on the way, then, huffing and puffing, I hurry to the end of a plushly-carpeted corridor.

Frederick's room is only a corner and a second corridor away, but the royal chef I bribed had tipped me off to the sentry on duty by his door. He had also told me - after he had drunk seven pints of Old Danish Beer - that a butler delivers a cup of hot milk to the prince every night at eleven o'clock on the dot.

Quickly, I find a bedroom just off the corridor. Thankfully, nobody is asleep in it and I creep in. There, I stop, and with my lips firmly clammed, I keep watch by the door.

A few moments later, a butler in a red tunic and carrying a tray and the all important cup of milk, scampers up the corridor.

The tip of my musket stops him short.

Beckoning him into the room, I rip off his tunic, bind him and stuff a hanky in his mouth.

'Listen to me, whatever your name is,' I tell the wide-eyed man, 'in a moment or two, I plan to royally offend your Danish prince. Sadly, for you anyway, he will probably blame you for allowing me to pinch your uniform. Now, I know and you probably know what a horrid fellow your boss is, so with this in mind I strongly suggest you jump on the next ship out of Copenhagen. I'm sorry I messed up your life here, but, hey, maybe this is a new beginning. Travel. See the world. Kill a dragon and marry a princess. Gotta be better than being a butler.'

Pulling on his tunic, I find to my annoyance it only just covers my elbows. The butler on the floor whimpers apologetically. Typical! He's only a foot taller than a dwarf. I had not thought of that.

I pull a red berry from my pocket. Botanists call it Actaea pachypoda or doll's eye; a potent little fellow and quick to act. I squeeze it over the cup. Now anybody who even sips the milk will sleep for a week. I snatch up the tray and pop the cup back on it. Then, squaring my shoulders, I step boldly out of the room and turn the corner.

'The prince enjoys his hot milk at eleven o'clock,' snaps

the sentry, 'not eleven ruddy thirty.' Snatching up the cup, he sniffs it. 'To put it mildly, he's not in the best of moods.'

'I'm new here,' I tell him warily. 'Just down from Sweden. I worked in the King's Castle in Stockholm and I tell you, I never had a problem there. Fewer corridors,' I answer his quizzical eyebrow.

'Got a little lost, hey?' He snorts. 'Well, you can't tell his lordship that. If you do, he'll probably lock you in irons and toss you in a cell.' He sips the milk and scowls.

'A new cow,' I quickly tell him. 'The chef told me she's from Scotland. Shetland, I think.'

'Hmm' He seems unconvinced. 'It's a bit flowery,' he murmurs. Instinctively, I feel for the pistol hidden on my belt but then his shoulders pop up in apathy. 'Go on in then,' his lips curl up wickedly, 'and if he throws a Ming vase at you, try to catch it or he'll dock you a year's pay.'

I swallow and muster a stiff nod. But with my hand on the door knob, I feel his fingers clamp my shoulder. 'Oh, and find a better uniform, preferably not a dwarf's.'

I nod feverently. 'Yes, yes, I will.' Boldly, I elbow open the door, cross my fingers and march in.

'You incompetent fool,' bellows Frederick. 'I'm dying here...' Then he sees who it is and his jaw drops to the top

button of his silk pyjamas.

The door slams shut and, calmly, I pull my musket from my belt. 'Hello, Sire.' The 'Sire' is drenched in scorn.

Prince Frederick in all his finery is lying on his bed, his old wolf, Skufsi Tennur, by his feet. It growls menacingly.

'Keep your furry pet where he is or I will put a bullet in your kneecap.' I say this softly but there is steel in my words.

Grinding his teeth, the prince grabs the wolf by the scruff of his neck.

'Sorry to intrude, Sire, but I'm here to collect my pay.' I spy the sword, Tyrfing, lying on a pillow on the end of his bed and I shuffle over to it. I pop the tray on a handy cabinet - oddly, identical to the 16th century French cabinet destroyed by the Germans in Le Moncelle - and unbuckle my own sword with my free hand. 'Here!' It clanks to the floor. 'Keep it.' Then I snatch up my prize.

A low growl erupts volcanically from the wolf. Or perhaps it was the prince.

'Now,' I smile wickedly and snap my fingers, 'the hundred kronor.'

A muscle jumps in his jaw. 'I'm in my bedchamber, you twit,' he snorts scornfully. 'I don't keep a chest of plundered silver under my bed springs.'

'The ring on your finger there, no, no, not your little pinky, the index finger. Good. Now, toss it here.'

'But, but,' splutters the prince, 'it was my Grandpa's.'

'And now it belongs to me,' I tell him coldly. Slowly and deliberately, I cock my pistol. 'Do it, Sire. NOW!'

With a hiss of fury, he pulls it off and lobs it to me. I catch it deftly. Then, quickly, I study it. Gold, set with two emeralds and a ruby the size of a small moon.

'Perfect,' I murmur, hypnotised by the glittery gems.

'This is - this is sheer folly, Major,' blusters Frederick.

I nod indolently. Undoubtedly, he will now try to stop me; offer me a job perhaps, a knighthood, or just try to bully me.

'I was told of your escape from Stockholm Hospital and the months you spent in London trying to find SWARM's HQ. Lord Gripenstedt is still after you, you know, the Swedish police too, and if you do this, if you choose to cross me, I too will hunt you for the rest of your days.' His eyes narrow to tiny slits. 'I will not stop till I see you in a box. Understood?'

It seems he went the 'bully' route.

'Perfectly, My Prince. But know this, I'm a devil to catch.'

Keeping a wary eye on Skufsi Tennur, I back pedal to the door.

'I allowed you to escape from Stockholm Hospital,' Frederick suddenly blurts out.

I stop and cock an eyebrow. What now?

'The sentry by the door; he left his post, yes? Very helpful of him. All you had to do was hobble up the corridor.'

'He went to the loo,' I say tersely.

'No, I bribed him, twenty kronor if I remember correctly, if he let you slip off.'

Sceptically, I chew on my lip. 'You left me there to be executed. Why, then, try to help me?'

'Truthfully,' he says the word slowly. Perhaps it is difficult for him; a word seldom on his lips, 'I was put up to it, by a very pretty lady.'

For a moment, I mull this over. The sentry had indeed deserted his bench by my door. But I also remember what Colonel Ludovic Fiquet told me in the hospital tent in France: '...he's a sly fox, tricky as a box of monkeys, so don't trust him...'

I decide to take the late-colonel's advice. 'Claptrap,' I sneer.

With a victory smirk, I yank open the door, not expecting the sentry I drugged to be slumped on it. He falls on my shoulder, knocking my musket from my hand.

'KILL HIM!' A bellow from Frederick.

The wolf springs off the bed and, with a snarl, sinks his teeth into the top of my calf. Frantically, I pull my new sword and I ruthlessly skewer the wild dog's chest.

A bolt of electricity floods my body. My mind is suddenly swamped with rocky valleys I do not know and snowy hills I never climbed. A mammoth tower of water erupts up and seems to almost hit the clouds. I see icy brooks and rocky cliffs, a waterfall thundering into a canyon, the swirling water meandering away in a hundred twists and turns.

Then, with the blurry eyes of a man awoken by a bucket of icy water, I, or whatever or whoever I now am, find myself in a cavern. It is pitch black, the sort of pitch black only children truly know of, the sort that looms over beds when trolls chuckle and plan mischief in the toy box.

But, oddly, I can still see.

The floor is strewn with skulls. I look to my feet, my paws, and try not to step on the ivory bone. There is a sheep's, a cow's, a, a...

OH MY GOD!

It is over in a second; a fuzzy memory of grey drawings.

I blink, my pulse slows and the wolf flops to the floor, splotching the carpet with blood.

WHAT THE...

WHAT THE HELL JUST HAPPENED!

I look dazedly to the Danish prince and in a poor attempt to cover my shock, I wink cheekily. 'Oops!' I mock him. 'I think I just killed your pet wolf.' My words judder and pitch from soprano to a deep tenor. 'You know, Sylva, my sister, she had a pet too. A hamster. A happy little critter with a lot fewer teeth.'

But Frederick seems totally unaffected by my jests. He is oddly composed now, almost smug in fact.

Unnervingly so.

I helter skelter down the corridor, a rather lazy yell of 'GUARDS!' chasing my flapping heels. Scrambling unceremoniously out of the window, I hurry over to the trees. There, I sprint over to the wall, snatch up the end of the rope and, hand over hand, pull myself up.

Thankfully, Blixt is exactly where I left him, so, with bullets ricocheting off the bricks, I jump, landing almost perfectly in the saddle.

'Giddy up!' I cry. I must get to a ship.

A speedy half hour later, I canter onto Copenhagen's docks. Hopping off my horse, I tow him over to a row of anchored ships. There, I spot a clipper and to my

#

astonishment I see it is the Flying Spur.

The clatter of hoofs is instantly answered by the thump in my chest. 'KEEP YOUR EYES OPEN, MEN!' A cry in the gloom. It must be a regiment of Frederick's troops.

I see the crew of the Flying Spur is already casting off. But what to do with my horse? There's no way I can get him on the ship, not with a bunch of Danish troopers on my heels.

I spy a boy fishing off the side of the wharf and by the look of his skinny body and tatty, patched-up trousers, he must be trying to catch his supper. 'Hey!' I holler. He looks up and I beckon him over. Pulling my rifle, my box of inks and my book from the saddle, I hand him Blixt's reins. 'If you can, try to sell him to a cavalryman. He's worth a pretty penny.'

The boy, I see, can hardly believe his good fortune and he thanks me profusely.

I look fondly on my old horse and gently rub his cheek. 'Goodbye, old pal,' I say softly. 'Enjoy the rest.'

Blixt's eyelids twitch and he stamps his hoof almost crushing my foot. I frown. Why, I wonder, is he suddenly so jumpy. Perhaps he knows I'm off and he's upset with me. 'Sorry,' I whisper to his trumpeting nostrils.

The Flying Spur is already six feet from the dock, but with a running jump, I land tidily on the deck.

My foot work must be improving.

Church, the ship's skipper, trots up to me, a musket in his paw.

'Hello, hello,' I chirrup cheerfully, offering him my hand.

'Major Tor!' He seems, well, almost happy to see me.

'So, where's the Flying Spur off to?' I ask him. 'Germany, Italy…?'

'China.'

'CHINA!'

I consider this for a moment. Well, I suppose the Crown Prince of Denmark, Stockholm's police constabulary and Lord Gripenstedt will find it awfully difficult to hunt for me on a different continent. Anyway, all my efforts to uncover the whereabouts of SWARM over the last twelve months have proved futile. And I do need a holiday.

The skipper rubs his chin in thought. 'The Flying Spur's still not got a cook.'

'You must be joking,' I chuckle. He eyes me coldly. He's not! 'But I only know Swedish food,' I protest. 'The crew will mutiny.'

'Major, this may surprise you to know, but it is very difficult to find a cook when word is the last fellow was impaled on a swordfish and tossed in the English Channel.'

211

'Oh, yes.' I shuffle my feet. 'Sorry.'

'Anyway, if you're the cook, there's a lot less chance of you murdering him,' Church comments dryly.

He's got a point. 'Where's the cat?' I ask him blankly. I don't know if I'm up to suffering six weeks of red welts.

'Prissy fell in love with a fat ginger in Shanghai. She jumped ship.' His shoulders droop sorrowfully. 'Where's the loyalty?'

Surrendering, I rally up a smile. 'A cook it is, Skipper.'

Hopping up on a handy barrel of rum, I roll up my trousers and study the bite on my calf; a memento of Skufsi Tennur's fury. The shock has left me now but I still wonder what it was I saw when the wolf bit me. Oddly, the wound is not particularly hurting and there is hardly a spot of blood. Odder still, for the first time in over a year the cut on my cheek is not throbbing and, despite being drenched in wolf blood, I'm not throwing up. I smile, wondering if perhaps Frederick's furry pet had magic teeth.

I follow Skipper Church's gaze; he is studying the twenty or so troopers swarming like angry bees over the docks. Looking for me, no doubt. 'They do not seem very happy,' he murmurs with a lopsided grin.

As it to prove it, a bullet zips by my cheek and thumps the

ship's wheel.

'Well, they did miss the last ferry to China,' I mumble flippantly back. I spot a man watching the Flying Spur from the very end of the dock. He is definitely not a Danish trooper, not with red bushy hair. I scowl, wondering who he is.

'Tell me, Major, what's on the menu for tomorrow?' chirrups the skipper. It seems not to bother him half the Danish army is trying to kill me. 'I did enjoy your spaghetti and your cherry-topped apple crumble.'

Wow! He remembers.

I ponder this for a second and then I punch him playfully on the shoulder, my mood lifting. 'A bloody lump of beef,' I tell him, grinning manically.

Suddenly, I feel chock-full of energy, like a barrel of Alfred Nobel's nitro-glycerine, the sparking fuse only a foot away, all set for my next explosive adventure.

Friday, 29th September, 1871
132 Days to Assassination Day

2205 hours, the Queen's Club, London

The Queen's Club is on Joy Street in London, only a stone throw away from Downing Street and the thunderous bell of Big Ben. In spite of the name, it is a 'men only' club, where lords, MPs and other men of influence meet to discuss politics and ways to swell their bank accounts.

The Gladstone Room is the finest, most opulent room in the club. Grandfather clocks tick pompously in the corners and cheetah furs litter the shiny polished floor. There is even a watercolour of Oxford, a Turner no less, over the crackling hickory log fire.

The room is usually very popular with the patrons of the elite club.

But not today.

Today, only two men sit in there enjoying a silver tray of cucumber rolls and lemon curd tarts. One of them is burly with beefy shoulders and a bulldog's jaw. His fingers look yellowish and tallowy as if they belong in a jar of embalming fluid. The second man is thinner with hands the size of shovels and a crown of red curls.

The rest of the gentlemen in the club keep away from them, unless they need the skills of a mutineer, a kidnapper - or a murderer.

The man with the carroty-red crown hops up from the sofa and steps over to the fire. There, he turns to warm his bottom. His code name is Mr Bee and he is a SWARM assassin with ninety-nine kills under his belt. He's very keen to hit a hundred. 'Sorry, Sir, but we,' he chews momentarily on his lower lip, 'I, lost him.'

'Lost him!?'

Squaring his shoulders, Mr Bee meets the other man's frosty eyes. He's his boss and his code name is Mr Spider. 'He jumped on a ship in Denmark, the Flying Spur.'

'Going to…?'

'China, My Lord. The port of Shanghai.'

'I see.' Thoughtfully, Spider puts a match to his tobacco-stuffed pipe.

Bee's eyes drift to the poker by his foot, his only weapon if his boss suddenly jumps up and attempts to batter him to a pulp. He's been told of Spider's temper; his legendary speed and agility, and how he always rewards his assassins when

they do not succeed. Granny Moth, he knows, still has scars; her reward for not succeeding in Sweden.

'I wonder why,' murmurs Spider. 'Major Tor's such a persistent sort of fellow and he's been on SWARM's heels in London now, for what, a year? I can't see him giving up.'

'All I know is he's a ruddy pest,' rasps Bee vindictively, 'and we need to swot him. You know, he's even been to Scotland Yard trying to get a copper there, an Inspector Jon Wayne, to help him.' He looks keenly to his boss. 'The new telegraph system is not working yet. Maybe in a month or two, but I can still send Granny Moth to China to instruct Mr Wasp to kill him. The Suez Canal is open now. The Goyo-Goyuku can be there in just over a month, two weeks prior to this old tug, the Flying Spur.'

'NO!' spits Spider. 'This is much too important a job for her. She messed up badly in Sweden. Gunpowder! Idiot woman. You need a ton of it to blow a hole in rice paper. Alfred Nobel and his nitro-glycerine is the future.' He eyeballs Bee sternly. 'No, you must go to China...'

'Me! But, Sir, the Karl Marx job in Germany is too important to just...'

'Yes, Mr Bee,' his words cut steel, 'you! Mr Mosquito can cover for you in Berlin. Do not fret; my plan will succeed.'

216

With narrow eyes, Spider puffs on his pipe. 'Tell Mr Wasp I wish for Tor to be schooled in Hornet Temple, in the art of the ninja. Just think, a trooper with his skills working for us. He will be a credit to SWARM.'

'Skills! HA! This dummy has no skills. He's just lucky.'

'Trust me, Mr Bee,' Spider smirks, a miser who just discovered a pebble is a golf nugget, 'he has now. I can feel it here,' he thumps his chest, 'in my blood. Anyway, we need new assassins; the blighter's murdered most of ours.'

'But...'

'Ant there's the Gladstone job to think of. Major Tor will be very handy for that. Do not forget, poor Madame Fiquet did sell her winery to pay for the hit; we do not want to upset her.'

Crushed, Bee stoops his brawny shoulders. Spider always has the final word. 'Yes, My Lord,' he mutters sullenly. 'But if the major says no to your kind offer?'

For a moment, Spider puffs thoughtfully on his pipe. Then his yellow-dyed eyes sharpen and he looks to Bee, his lips curled up wickedly. 'Then tell my old chum, Mr Wasp, Tor murdered Mr Grasshopper, his only brother - with a swordfish.'

2205 hours, The Flying Spur, the Atlantic, just off Lisbon, Portugal

I cannot sleep.

My mind is cluttered with cheetah furs and the thick bushy eyebrows of Alfred Nobel. I see a tomb sculpted in ivory-white marble, Andrew Ducrow etched in the waxy bricks, and a cucumber roll in the jaws of a wolf, his paws peppered black...

Dropping my otter pelt blanket to the cabin floor, I reluctantly clamber off my hammock, pull on my tunic and amble old-mannishly up the steps to the deck of the Flying Spur. The wind, it seems, also cannot sleep, twisting in her bed, intent on snapping the masts in two. I spy Compass Cob, the ship's navigator, on the wheel, battling to keep the clipper bow-on to the watery knolls. I wave cheerily; I hardly ever throw up nowadays, even in the storms.

So...

I tuck my hand in my armpits.

...I'm off to China!

The land of emperors and the Chinese cracker flower; and my Grandmother Toyi's home. I just hope the ghosts of the men I lost will not follow me there. My sigh is whipped from my lips by the squalling wind. I know the memory of Gurli will; and the abhorrence I feel for Granny Moth and SWARM.

Even now, so far from my problems, I wonder who Spider is. Duke Solbakken's impostor had told me he had seen my face. But what I want to know is, had I seen his? I also wonder where in London SWARM's HQ is hidden. I had looked for almost twelve months with no luck, not even with the help of Scotland Yard. But what annoys me the most, what keeps me from my sleep, is not knowing why the assassins attempted to murder everybody at the party and not just the Swedish monarch. This puzzle runs endlessly in a loop in my mind. It is important. I don't know why, but it is.

I look up to the sky for answers. Clusters of stars hang like lemons in a tree and the moon is full, soft as snow…

Suddenly, a tidal wave of hurt slams into me. I clutch for my stomach, my teeth clamped over a paltry whimper. It is torture, as if there's a wild dog in there chewing on my liver.

'Welcome to my pack, Major Tor.' The words echo in my skull, ricocheting off the walls like the cry of a banshee. Oddly, for a second, perhaps even two, they comfort me. Then...

four...

ominous...

words...

'I OWN YOU NOW!'

My blood turns cold. Slowly, I sink to the deck, my knees up to my chin.

BOOM!

A second 'knock out' blow and a volcano of pitiless fury erupts in my body. My chin snaps up, my jaws fly open and my eyes hunt frantically for the moon.

They find it and with untold ferocity...

I HOWL!

Billy Bob Buttons

Evil needs only
a timid victim

TOR
WOLF RISING
book two of the TOR trilogy

BILLY BOB BUTTONS

TIFFANY SPARROW

SPOOK SLAYER

32703722R00130

Printed in Great Britain
by Amazon